Surviving the Zombies is an excellent book to start you on your preparations; Frank has shared in great detail what you must do to protect your family; not just what to use; but the how and why is explained!

— **PAMELA CARROLL,**
Noted Survivalist

Think you know zombies? Think again. Read Frank Borelli's *Surviving the Zombies* for a comprehensive look at their origins, and how you can ensure their demise. Frank knows Zombies.

— **JOHN M. WILLS,**
Award-winning author and reviewer
at the New York Journal of Books.

This is a work of fiction that really makes you think, "Wow, this really could be what happens!" It puts a very realistic spin on the zombie frenzy and will make you stop and think... exactly how prepared are you?

— **STEPHANIE BIBB,**
Zombie Apocalypse Survivalist

OTHER BOOKS BY FRANK BORELLI

*"American Thinking: Sustaining The Warrior Values That
Made American Strong – And Still Can!!"*
Published 2006

"American Thinking II: Americans Make America Strong"
Published 2010

"Father to Son: Guidance in Following the Straight & Narrow"
Published February 2011

"Above Dirt: Motivational Thoughts Supporting A Positive Outlook"
With Steve Forgues
Published January 2011

"Personal Disaster Planning Handbook"
Published June 2012

Surviving the
ZOMBIES
THINGS THE CDC DIDN'T KNOW

Frank Borelli

Responder Media books may be ordered through booksellers or by contacting:

Responder Media
1663 Liberty Drive
Bloomington, IN 47403
www.respondermedia.com
1-(877) 444-0235

Because of the dynamic nature of the Internet, any web addresses or links contained in this book may have changed since publication and may no longer be valid. The views expressed in this work are solely those of the author and do not necessarily reflect the views of the publisher, and the publisher hereby disclaims any responsibility for them.

Certain stock imagery © Thinkstock.
Any people depicted in stock imagery provided by Thinkstock are models, and such images are being used for illustrative purposes only.

ISBN: 978-1-4705-0011-5 (e)
ISBN: 978-1-4705-0010-8 (sc)

Library of Congress Control Number: 2012915219

Printed in the United States of America

Responder Media rev. date: 9/5/2012

ACKNOWLEDGEMENTS

While I'd like to say that the idea for this book was wholly and purely my own, it would be a bold-faced lie. Prior to starting on this book, I finished a disaster planning handbook, and a friend of mine made the observation that most of the preparation I espoused would be as applicable in a zombie apocalypse as they are for hurricanes, earthquakes and economic collapse. That set part of the idea for this book – how to prepare to survive and thrive in the midst of a zombie outbreak.

Then I had a conversation with another friend of mine, Mr. Chuck Buis, and mentioned that it was his fault I even thought about zombies anyway because he had so aggressively recommended a particular book to read a couple years ago. I mentioned that I was considering writing my own zombie survival book and he immediately started spouting title suggestions. To say that he liked the idea would be an understatement. Chuck was motivated enough about it for me to get motivated about it, and you are reading the results. Thank you, Mr. Buis, for your enthusiasm and the title suggestions. I ended up pretty close to the mark.

As I was writing, I was constantly seeing posts about zombies in my Twitter feed and on my Facebook page from friends. One friend in particular, Dawn Brown, is a zombie fanatic – and that might not be wording it strongly enough. Dawn also has a background in literature though and volunteered her editing services on the condition that she'd get a copy of the book prior to publication. As things worked out, she got the book piecemeal as I wrote it, and she edited it along the way, sending me back those edits which I worked in as I continued writing. Dawn, thank you very much for your energy and enthusiasm, not to mention your editing work. I've never seen anyone so eager to receive emails with draft manuscript bits and pieces attached. I've also never seen anyone (else) design and bake zombie cupcakes, but that's just one of the things that make you who you are.

As always, I have to thank my family. My children – every last one of them – chuckled softy when dad announced he was writing a zombie survival book. After they finished laughing, they all had an idea or three to share. My wife kind of shook her head and said, "Whatever you can sell." This will be my seventh published book, and I'm not getting rich on royalties (yet) so I think she views my writing as an outlet for my otherwise nonproductive but overactive imagination.

Finally, thank you to the readers. Yes, writing does relieve an itch of sorts. Sometimes authors are simply driven to get the words and story out onto "paper." Still, if no one reads it and offers feedback (which we always hope will be positive), then writing is only partially fulfilling. So thank you to all of you as well.

Read on. I hope you thoroughly enjoy.

CONTENTS

FOREWORD

Few people that I've met are so willing to open their mouths, share a thought and not care if others laugh at them. As the zombie pandemic started and spread, those who spoke of it typically did so only in apparent jest; only couched as a joke; only presented in a completely non-serious way... lest they be thought mentally cracked or simply stupid.

I was one of those people in the nineties who recognized the threat; took to the planning and preparation with gusto and kept myself mentally and emotionally strong through all of the insults, criticisms and society's derision of who I was and what I was doing.

Of course, that changed when even the leaders of the world's governments started to panic as a result of the zombie pandemic. All of a sudden I had those world leaders sending representatives to offer me huge sums of worthless paper they called money to teach their militaries how to fight the zombie infestation that was spreading beyond their ability to contain it – or even just the information about it.

Prior to that, I met a guy in a bar. It was late one evening and I was tipping up a cold bottle of beer, hoping the flavor of hops and barley would help clear my sinuses of the smell of rotted flesh from the zombie I had just destroyed. The guy approached me with confidence, but also carefully; as if he wasn't sure what my reaction to his approach would be. His words were simple. "I know what you did. I know why you did it. I want you to teach me and every member of my family what we need to know to survive what's coming."

There was no smile on his face. There was nothing about his body language that indicated he might be joking even the slightest bit. I perceived him as 100% serious. He didn't offer me money. He didn't ask what I wanted to be paid. He offered me belief and the reassurance that if I trained his family they'd welcome me and support my efforts as long as I fought beside them to protect them when the time came; when the pandemic really exploded and things got uglier than any movie or book had ever shown.

I took him at his word and we shook hands. He bought me another beer and tipped his own – the first and last beer I'd ever see him drink – as we started down the path of basic planning.

THIS is his story. HE learned to survive. Some of the lessons weren't easy. I'M still around – so that's a hint that I might have a clue what I'm doing too. As someone who has been touted "the world's most experienced zombie destroyer," I highly recommend you read this book; study the materials; embed the lessons in your daily life. Quite frankly, it's the only way you'll survive when the next zombie pandemic occurs.

Travis Anvil Stone
Noted zombie destroyer of the early 21st century

INTRODUCTION

Zombie[1]:

- ❀ The body of a dead person given the semblance of life but mute and will-less.
- ❀ A person whose behavior or responses are wooden, listless, or seemingly rote; automaton.

Dead[2]:

- ❀ No longer living; deprived of life.
- ❀ Not endowed with life; inanimate.
- ❀ Resembling death; deathlike.
- ❀ Bereft of sensation; numb.

Undead[3]:

- ❀ No longer alive but animated by a supernatural force.

In the early 21st century, zombies and all things related exploded into popular culture. Although there had been some successful movies created about them in the late 20th century, the rate of mention of zombie-related topics really increased over 1000% between the years 1995 and 2010. Seemingly out of the blue there were books, movies, posters, blogs, toys, clothing and even weapons designed or created depicting zombies or a zombie related purpose. As an example, if you searched the word "zombie" on the popular website "Amazon.com" you'd receive more than 2,200 items back; and that didn't include related searches that were just ambiguous enough to not be included in that single word search return.

Little did the general world population know that this saturation of society with zombie information and materials was intentionally done by a cabal of world leaders, much like the flood of science-fiction information and materials between the years 1965–1995; much like the flood of end-of-the-world information and materials between the years 1990–2005. In fact, the zombie fascination seemed, at one point, merely an extension of the end-of-the-world scenarios that simply put a metaphysical twist on the basic fear of the end of our world.

But now, looking back at the events in recent years, it becomes obvious that many world leaders – whether they were elected or they were dictators – simply wanted to plant the idea firmly into the community psyche of their respective populations so that if, on the off chance, a zombie "apocalypse" occurred, the population would be more receptive to government control; the removal of basic liberties and freedoms in the interest of "the greater good."

History and experience gift us with better perspective. It is one thing to look forward at a fictional future possibility of the "living dead" or the "walking undead" or (more simply) "zombies" growing in numbers so as to threaten the majority of the world's population. It is an entirely different thing to find out that it's happening… that it's BEEN happening and that not only have the world's leaders conspired to hide the truth but that they fully intended to use that truth to increase their chokehold of power.

This is the story of one man and his family as they struggled to survive the zombie pandemic that swept the globe. In truth, the first infections were seen in 2010 and 2011, and by the time the infamous "end of the world" date of December 21, 2012, came around, the general populations of the world – those who paid attention anyway – were becoming suspicious. The smart ones were already planning and preparing. The really smart ones realized that if they were right about the unthinkable – a zombie pandemic – that it wouldn't just happen ONCE. Anything that happens once can happen again.

So, I type their story as they shared it with me. Interspersed in the chapters of their experience are the lessons intelligent people have learned; some based on information disseminated by the government agencies of the various world powers, others based on simple common sense and ugly experience.

I encourage you to read their story and study the lessons in between. Because it's happened once… are you willing to bet your life and the lives of those you love that it will never happen again?

Frank Borelli
Written from Stormhaven – location protected

ZOMBIES IN HISTORY

As we contemplate the "zombie in history," we need to take into consideration the definitions and expand our minds some. Any time you plan a defense (or offense) against an enemy, you must know them. You must know their strengths and weaknesses as well as your own. But you must know the truth of them. Wars across the ages have been lost due to bad intelligence. Let's take a moment and identify what we are NOT dealing with in this book and then we can clearly identify what we ARE dealing with.

As defined in the introduction, "dead" is dead. No life. No movement. No animation. We are NOT concerned with the dead. In fact, thanks to the quirk of chemistry that drives zombies to only crave LIVING tissue, the dead are of no concern at all. As we'll discuss later at some point, the sentimental drive we humans have to dispose in some ceremonial way of our dead can cost us dearly during any kind of zombie infestation or outbreak. Let the dead be. You can't do anything for them. Nature will reclaim them. History has proven that zombies will leave the dead alone; nothing living there to feast on.

Also as defined in the introduction, "undead" is a word used to identify a larger group of targets than we want to specify when discussing zombies. As examples, the "undead" would include reanimated mummies, vampires, artificially animated creatures, etc.

None of the zombie events reported throughout history include the undead in any variation; however, in some cases, the mummies of zombies have been identified, and there may be some valuable lessons to learn from the preparation of them for interment.

If you believe some popular reports and/or publications, then the oldest documented zombie outbreak occurred in Katanda, Central Africa in approximately 60,000 BC[4]. An archaeological dig revealed 13 crushed Homo sapiens skulls accompanied by nearby piles of ash. The skulls were carbon dated to estimate their age and the ash was chemically tested to prove that it was the burned remains of Homo sapiens. Nearby cave drawings eerily depict bi-pedal humanoid figures walking in the now-familiar slow-moving-arms-raised zombie manner. Perhaps more incriminating is the fact that those "zombie" figures had other obviously human figures in their mouths.

Moving forward in history, we find the next documented zombie outbreak not occurring until some 57,000 years later (give or take a millennia) in Egypt[5]. That's still on the

African continent so it's not difficult to understand how it could have happened. Dormant virus strains have proven to carry effectiveness across spans of time greater than those we can measure with contemporary medical technology – simply because the virus has been alive yet dormant longer than the technology has existed. Knowing that, it's a reasonable assumption that the zombie-making virus lay dormant but alive and was somehow reactivated when that next breakout is recorded. In this case, the discovery was made inside a tomb but outside its crypt. The mummified body showed human bite marks on one arm and the inside of the tomb was covered with scratch marks. Based on the decomposition of the bio-material left in the stone from those scratches, forensic archaeologists estimated that the scratches were made over a period of years. With no sign of food storage vessels nor of human waste inside the tomb, only one conclusion can be reached. Further examination of the remains revealed signs of a previously unidentified virus currently called Solanum – also know as "the zombie virus." (Readers should note that this virus has many variants and there is debate even amongst the most experienced medical personnel as to whether Solanum by itself can cause zombieism or if another contributing factor must be present).

The next documented events occurred in 500 BC and 329 BC[6]. The first of the two was in Africa (again) with the second being in Afghanistan. Given the land mass connections between the African continent and that of what is now called the Middle East, it again is not a stretch of any imagination to see the virus traveling in a host – alive but dormant.

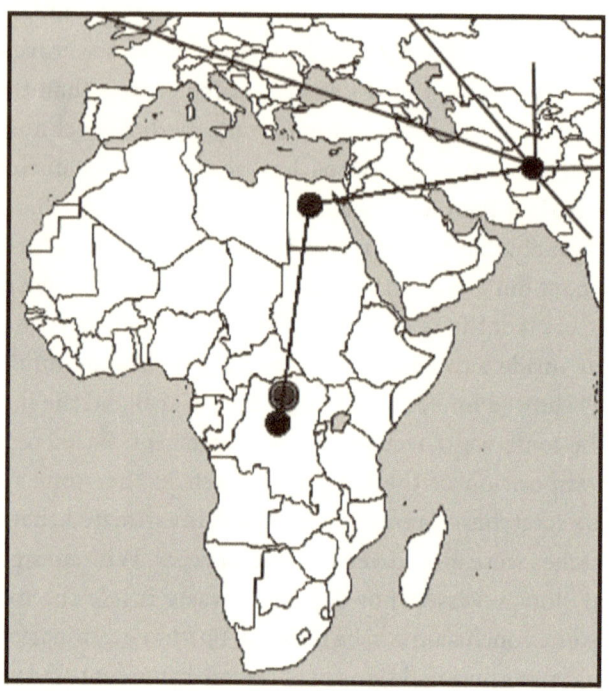

What marks the event in Afghanistan as unique is the apparent reproduction and spread of the virus from that point. If you look at the provided map with the first four outbreaks or events marked, you can see a relative line of travel; however, after the event in Afghanistan in 329 BC, the next events are quite spread out: China, Scotland, Algeria, Germany, France... It is almost as if the original virus was traveling in a single host who then infected several others traveling divergent paths out from Afghanistan.

Curiously, Alexander the Great had arrived in Afghanistan just one year before the recorded outbreak. It is entirely possible – though not provable with current information

– that when Alexander the Great left Afghanistan after his brief sojourn there, some member or members of his army took the virus with them out of Afghanistan. Alexander himself would live only another six years before dying in Babylon – what is in present day Iraq. Prior to his death, records show that Alexander had clearly pressed his armies into India – a hop, skip and a jump from China. Members of his party – representatives of his empire - had traveled the width and depth of Europe. Alexander's military might may well have been a contributing factor in the ready spread of any virus or other contributing factor for zombieism.

It wasn't until the year 1253 AD that zombieism appears to have left the eastern edge of the Atlantic Ocean. According to records in the Icelandic national archives, an Icelandic Chieftain named Gunnjborn Lundergaart had established a village that had been ravaged by an unknown force. Having left the village, when Lundergaart returned with his sailing crew, they found the village of 153 decimated; the remains of about three dozen villagers identifiable and three "people" still alive – or at least mobile. These three were described as two women and one child, all of whom appeared wounded without blood loss, decomposed without sign of rot, and grayish in coloration. As the three approached Lundergaart and his crew, giving no reply to attempts at communication, they were seen as a threat and promptly hacked apart by the massive Icelandic swords of that era. Lundergaart ordered all of the remains – of the three "people" and the dead villagers – burned. Also in the report it says that Lundergaart ordered himself killed, dismembered and burned as well so that he could join his family in the hereafter.

This report is of great importance because it is the first to show that the virus had spread into a climate that can be severely cold. Whether or not the zombies can function in freezing temperatures is a different concern (and discussed at a later point). That the virus causing zombieism CAN survive, dormant but alive, in temperatures documented (in Iceland and Greenland) well below zero (Fahrenheit) presents a ready danger to travelers in those climes.

Following the outbreak on Greenland, there were several more across the span of the next approximately 130 years ranging in location from Asia to Central and then South America and another outbreak in a frozen area of our planet: Siberia. The Siberian outbreak in the year 1583 was just as ignored as the one in Greenland, both of them serving as strong indicators that:

1) The zombie causing virus/bacteria/condition is not killed by sub-freezing temperatures, and

2) Zombies themselves can function at sub-freezing temperatures at least for some period of time.

(This is significant information and should be noted carefully. Part of the misinformation disseminated by the CDC was that zombies could be easily frozen at temperatures between zero and thirty-two degrees Fahrenheit, thereby rendering them harmless. Not only is it next to impossible to freeze them, the cold does NOT stop or slow the spread of the zombie virus.)

The other significant lesson learned in the Siberian outbreak was that zombie flesh, if consumed, is fatal to the person or people who eat(s) it. Cannibalism is a dead practice amongst civilized society anyway, but in times of extreme hardship, people do odd things that they wouldn't normally even consider doing. In the case of the Siberian outbreak, there was no food available, and the party in question – composed of several men – dug up, cooked and ate bodies from the village they were in. ONE of those bodies happened to be that of a zombie female, and every man who consumed her flesh – even cooked – died a painful death. One man in the party was bitten before she was cut up and cooked, and he too died – only to reanimate the next day.

The final lesson from the Siberian outbreak was how long it can take for a zombie to actually freeze beyond function in sub-freezing temperatures. According to reports, the reanimated bitten/infected man revived after a night (approximately 12 hours) and then took nearly a full day (24 hours) to freeze beyond function. That's not to say that he was "dead" again or that he didn't present any threat. His flesh was merely too cold to be mobile based on the neurological commands his nervous system was sending out in compliance with the zombie virus drive.

The first report of a zombie outbreak in North America allegedly occurred in the lost colony of Roanoke Island, North Caroline in the year 1587. American Indian lore claims that some colonists from Roanoke Island went hunting in a cursed part of the forest, encountered zombies, were attacked and infected before returning to their community. Once those infected hunters died and were reanimated, they became a threat both to the colony and to the American Indians in the area. To protect their own best interests, the American

Indians attacked and decimated the zombie colonists along with anyone who had come into contact with them and then burned the bodies for guaranteed eradication of the outbreak. It's important to note that while this is the first reported outbreak in North America, it obviously couldn't be. If the Indians knew what the problem was; recognized it; identified it and knew how to fight/eradicate it, then they had obviously come into contact with zombies before.

The next almost three hundred years saw outbreaks in Asia, southern Atlantic islands, the Caribbean and Europe as well as both South and East Africa. Nothing significant was to be learned from those outbreaks except that the zombie virus had spread world wide and every country; every state; every community needed to be aware of the potential threat and ready to counter it.

In 1848, the next outbreak occurred in North America, but as interesting as it was, there is a far more compelling piece of information to share. We'll get back to the 1848 outbreak in Owl Creek Mountains, Wyoming in a moment.

As we examine the timeline of zombie outbreaks, we see that from approximately 60,000 B.C. to 1848 A. D. there are 25 documented zombie outbreaks. That's 25 across a span of 61,848 years – or approximately one (on average) every 2,474 years. Obviously the average is FAR off since there was such a huge gap between the earliest outbreaks, but you see the point.

From 1848 to present, there have been 35 documented outbreaks. That's 35 outbreaks in 164 years or an average of one every 4.7 years. What's the lesson? *Zombie outbreaks are becoming more and more prevalent, and if you aren't preparing to survive the next one, then you are, by default, planning on being a zombie's dinner.* Have I got your attention now? Sit up and pay attention.

In 1848 in the Owl Creek Mountains of Wyoming, two hunters came across a group which had been stranded in a ravine with walls too steep to climb out of and no other means of escape. The nine men and women were observed to be standing facing the walls of the ravine without movement at all. According to the hunters' report, they all appeared "grayish in color as if their bodies were covered by ash" but their clothing didn't look overly worn or dirty. The zombie campers didn't respond verbally when the hunters called down to them but DID begin trying to climb the sheer ravine walls to get to the hunters.

Noticing the odd behavior of the camping party zombies and receiving absolutely no verbal response – or even eye contact – from the zombies stuck in the ravine, the hunters refrained from lowering a rope or attempting any sort of rescue. Instead they called in the local authorities and, upon seeing what the situation was, the local authorities evacuated the area prior to – as far as anyone can ascertain – shooting each camper zombie in the head. According to the last written record of this event, heaps of wood, leaves and any other material that would burn were dropped on top of the zombies in the ravine and lit on fire. Nothing but ash remained after the blaze burned itself out.

This is the biggest part of the experience that we need to heed: ONE of the local authorities had breathed in the smoke from the burning zombie bodies and it was fatal. He died two days later, was reanimated one day after that and was promptly shot in the head by another local authority. The body was thrown into the ravine where the other zombies had been burned. It too was burned, and everyone involved made a hasty escape from the flames and smoke once the fire was lit. Pay attention: whatever virus causes zombieism IS NOT destroyed by fire, dryness, moisture, sub-freezing temperatures, etc. Take all necessary precautions to protect yourself from exposure in any way. It's not just the zombie bite that can infect you; it's ingestion of it in any form.

(This is another piece of misinformation that the CDC has disseminated: destroying infection by fire has long been thought to be effective. It does not destroy the zombie virus.)

The only continent that has not seen a zombie outbreak to date is Antarctica. It is the opinion of the author that this lack of outbreak is NOT due to the inability of the zombie virus to survive such extreme cold temperatures. Instead, I believe that there have simply been too few people there for sufficient mass to occur for an outbreak to become possible. Think of it this way: if one in every 500,000 people are infected - are carriers of the virus - and only 10,000 people have been to Antarctica, then it will be several hundred more years before enough folks have gone there that the chance will be great enough that even ONE of them will be a carrier.

Since 1848, outbreaks have occurred on every continent and on several island chains. The most concentrated outbreaks occurred in California between the years 1992 and 1994. With five documented outbreaks in that time frame, California – between the Joshua Tree National Forest and Santa Monica

Bay – is documented as having the highest risk of outbreak and, therefore, the highest risk of infection for residents.

If you live in any part of southern California, the Baja Peninsula or even the western sections of Nevada or Arizona, you probably ought to consider relocating if you're worried about zombie outbreaks. If you decide to stay where you are, it's recommended that you double up on all plans and preparations just to be safe.

2

I USED TO NOT CARE
ABOUT ZOMBIES

I remember a time when "the cold war" was our biggest worry. School drills had us getting under our desks, covering our heads and not looking at any flash from an atomic bomb – as if any of that would have done any good. If you were going to be ash, you were going to be ash. There were two documented zombie outbreaks in the world in the 1950s.

Then I remember that the biggest problem facing society was unequal civil rights. Differences in how we treated people of different races, gender, age, financial status… it all became one big challenge as we tried to treat everyone equally. The problem was that everyone may have been born equal, but they didn't grow equal. Some people took advantage of opportunities; some people worked hard; some people didn't. Nowhere did laziness punish people more than in a zombie outbreak – but most of society was ignorant of the threat in the 1960s. There were three documented zombie outbreaks in the world in the

1960s, and one of them occurred in Eastern Laos – right across the border from…

Then there was Vietnam and the oil shortage. Do you know how many reported zombie outbreaks there were during the Vietnam war anywhere in Vietnam? NONE. How can that be? The zombie virus was almost assuredly there. A reported outbreak occurred across the border in Laos in 1968. Cannibalism was documented as occurring in many of the small villages. Brain infections, muscle tissue infections, digestive tract infections… they were all documented. How is it that not a single zombie outbreak was recorded? All I'm going to say is that's what happens when the military controls all information coming out of a given geographic region. There was no Internet back then, and news reporters had to ask permission from the military to go anywhere. It certainly made information control easier. During the 1970s, as America ended its involvement in Vietnam and tried to settle things within its own borders, there were three zombie outbreaks documented world wide; two in Africa and one in the United States.

Then came the 1980s and a relative calm before the storm. Even as America tried to recover from the challenges of the late '60s and all of the '70s, relative peace ruled the land. That didn't stop a zombie outbreak in Arizona in '84… There were a total of four zombie outbreaks documented world wide in the '80s.

The 1990s should have opened a lot of eyes… but we humans seemed bound and determined to ignore any threat we can. We were too happy with a successful (short) war in the Middle East in the early 1990s, and in 1999 we were either getting ready to party like Prince had said we should in his song or we were planning for the end of the world as we knew it when computers failed world wide at the turn of the millennium.

We should have opened our eyes to real – not imagined – threats. While the world didn't crash at midnight as our calendar changed from 1999 to 2000, we could look back at no less than seven zombie outbreaks in the decade we called "the '90s." FIVE of them were in the United States. ALL five of those were in California.

In 2001 there was a single outbreak recorded in Europe.

In 2002 there was a single outbreak recorded in the U.S. Virgin Islands.

In 2003 the United Nations held a special meeting to discuss "weapons of mass destruction." Leaked reports indicated that what was really discussed was the zombie pandemic that was barely cut off in California in the 1990s and a working agreement on containment world wide to keep a true zombie pandemic from kicking off.

Yeah… through all that I could have cared less about zombies. I was almost one myself. Not literally… but mentally. I read what I was fed in the newspapers. I watched what I was fed on TV. I listened to what I was fed on the radio. I read what I was fed as I surfed the Internet. It was all pretty much the same. Economic turmoil. Social status disagreements. Countries at war. Terrorist attacks. Near world wide economic collapse. Civil unrest as greedy people accused greedy people of not sharing what they were all greedy for.

In the summer of 2012, a new form of "zombie" was seen, but it was sensationalized in a big way by the major news services. Up and down the east coast, and a few times in the Midwest, people on drugs began eating pieces of other people; occasionally they killed them first. There was the guy in Florida who ate another man's face off and didn't seem to notice it much when the police shot him several times. Then there was the guy in Maryland who killed a woman and then ate her brains and heart. Several other similar incidents were recorded in just a couple of months that summer. While these weren't true zombie occurrences, the mainstream media hyped up the "zombie" side of each event and zombie fever continued to grow.

I was kind of into the preparedness movement that grew in the late 1990s and early part of the 21st century. I stocked some food; made sure my ammo supplies were maintained. Every payday I bought a 100-round box of ammo for my .45, a 20-round box of ammo for my .30-.30 and a 25-round box for my twelve gauge. I steadily built up my store of ammo. I had the ability to store about 150 gallons of water and, more importantly, the ability to purify it to make it safe. I kept about 100 gallons of gasoline stored and stabilized "just in case." Plenty of my friends laughed at me even as I wrote a handbook on how to plan and prepare for disasters. Little did I know at that time the disaster I was planning and preparing for.

Then came the day when all hell broke loose – at least as I perceived it. Literally. I was watching a news story about some protestors in a park in New York City and a cameraman had captured what everyone thought was a costumed protestor moving slowly out of the park and toward the crowd. It was near Halloween. No one appeared to think much about the shabby suit, tussled hair, gray skin and slowly moving pace… arms raised as if aiming or guiding him.

The first protestor he got to actually laughed, commented on his costume, hammed it up for the camera… and then screamed as the "costumed protestor" grabbed him, pulled him in and bit him on the face. The camera caught it all, live on national television, as a chunk of the man's cheek was bitten clean off, the wound bleeding freely and the "costumed protestor" chewing up the chunk – still "live" on camera and being broadcast nationwide.

On camera pandemonium broke out. Other protestors came to the rescue of the bitten guy. The zombie – no longer being viewed as a protestor in a good costume, but as an obvious threat to everyone within reach – was pretty much beaten to the ground. He was nearly smashed to a pulp to be honest with you. He was knocked down, punched, kicked and stomped until he was a mess of tissue on the ground.

Thankfully some of the protestors had been violent enough to crush his skull as they stomped him with their boots. Unfortunately for many, bits and pieces of his infected flesh were thrown around; splattered about; transmitted via contact to several of those involved.

The next morning brought us news about the bitten man's death and the illness that seemed to be killing several of the others involved. Several newscasters reported that the "zombie" was just another drugged out freak; one more in the chain of them we'd seen in recent news.

Then the news blackout came. Suddenly the hospital was quarantined; the Center for Disease Control and the World Health Organization took over. A National Guard unit out of Wyoming was activated and assigned to cordon off a four square block area around the hospital. Every building within that area was evacuated.

Huge amounts of money were spent by New York City and New York State and the federal government to sterilize every square inch inside that four square block area. No one was allowed in except CDC and WHO workers. The news showed footage of a New York City cop who tried to get in and was shot by a National Guardsman. What startled most, I think, was that the Guardsman didn't issue any warning; didn't shoot the officer in the chest as television had conditioned us to expect; just like we'd expect the cop's vest to stop the bullet even though, in reality, it never would. What startled everyone was the calm precise way the National Guardsman raised his rifle, took careful aim, and shot the cop right between the eyes.

Within a few minutes a couple CDC and WHO folks in full infection protective gear came out, gathered up the cop's body and took it back inside the quarantined area. It had all been captured by a news helicopter that was circling the area. Using one heck of a zoom lens, the 'copter news crew had captured clear video of the cop approaching, not stopping as he got close, the National Guardsman shooting him and the health workers coming to collect the carcass. It was a reality check for everyone watching.

I knew when I saw that news coverage that something ugly was coming. I wasn't sure what it was or when it would arrive, but I knew for sure and certain that I was glad I'd been stockpiling ammo. I immediately set about filling all my water storage containers and insuring the security of my home. I double checked my supply of thick plastic – both black and clear – and my rolls of duct tape (20 rolls).

The very next day a statement was released by a representative of the CDC explaining away the National Guardsman's actions by describing the highly contagious not-yet-identified virus that had infected a number of protestors. It was described as "ebola-like" but even more deadly. The CDC representative went on to explain that every protestor who had come in contact with "patient zero," as they were then calling the first zombie captured on live television, had died. Strict procedures and protocols were in place to contain the virus and everyone's cooperation was necessary.

Nothing else came out of the four square block area for the next three days. America and the world had almost gotten back to normal as much as the average person could tell. Then another news chopper circling the quarantined area in New York caught video tape of a number of people coming out of the hospital heading toward the quarantine boundary. They looked, on film, as if they were moving slow and in an uncoordinated fashion. Some had their arms raised; some just looked like they were out for an afternoon stroll. Some were dressed in patient gowns (lots of gray butt showing) while some were in hospital scrubs like doctors and nurses wear. Some were in security uniforms... some were naked.

When the first National Guardsman saw them coming, it was like déjà vu. He raised his rifle, took careful aim and shot the person closest to him as the person approached. Again, live on national television, the country watched as the person's head snapped back from the impact of the round and, even on television, you could see the spray of brain, bone, hair and tissue as it splattered out the back of the person's head. Without a pause the National Guardsman moved his sights to the next person… fired again… more spray… another body fell.

As I watched – and others I've spoken with since then agree with me – I kept waiting for the people walking out of the hospital to panic, turn and run back in. They never did. They never would. It was later revealed that every person in the hospital and inside the quarantine area had eventually been infected, died, was reanimated and became part of what's become known as "the zombie nation."

Of course, at the time we had no way of knowing. We were all news-zombies ourselves. We just watched, listened to the mainstream media talking heads criticize the news blackout from the government. We listened as they criticized the National Guardsmen. We watched as a "civil rights leader" got his fifteen minutes of fame calling for congressional investigations into everyone and anyone he thought might have been responsible for that Guardsman pulling the trigger.

A whole new team of scientists and doctors from the CDC and WHO were flown in. It took less than twelve hours from the first shot to when a new National Guard unit was on station as well. The first National Guard unit – the unit that had, at that time, done all the shooting – was transported to the Marine Corps base on Guantanamo Bay, Cuba where they were kept in strict isolation for a week. Rumors surfaced that they had been infected and were being isolated until either a cure could be found or they ended up executed just like they'd executed the infected people coming out of the hospital. Little did we all know.

All of them were released a week later. None of them reported having been treated badly. All of them reported having undergone blood tests, drug tests (urinalysis), having DNA samples taken (saliva, skin and bone marrow samples). All of them reported having had shavings taken from their fingernails and toenails (no pain involved; just shallow shavings for collection and analysis). Each of them had received a complete physical along with full body MRI scans and a full set of X-rays. They were all given a clean bill of health and released. Upon their release, a four-star general got on television and said that he was glad to report that the viral infection in New York City had been completely contained; that he was saddened at the loss of life that had occurred; that he was encouraged by the outpouring of support the military had received from our country's citizens.

I wasn't sure what he was talking about. I hadn't heard anyone support, what appeared on television to be, the cold-blooded assassinations of multiple hospital staff members, doctors, nurses, orderlies, patients and security personnel. I had heard condemnation; I heard demands for explanation. I had read "Letters to the Editor" in a number of newspapers calling for congressional investigations of the National Guard Bureau and the command staff for the first unit that had been on station. I never heard anyone voice any support. I guess that's what they call "spin" on television… and in politics.

Within the month, though, similar incidents occurred in Chicago, Los Angeles, Houston, Memphis, Birmingham, Cheyenne, Las Vegas, Philadelphia and Washington, DC. Around the world outbreaks occurred in places like Berlin, Paris, Rome (it's almost humorous to look back at the reaction of the Vatican to a zombie outbreak but maybe we'll get to that later). Vancouver, Sydney, Rio, Mexico City... all of a sudden, seemingly out of the blue, zombies were everywhere – but no one was calling them that, and the world "leaders" steadily tried to use the outbreaks as a way to increase their stranglehold on the citizens of their countries. Where dictatorships and tyrannies already existed, things got worse. Where democracy still thrived – or just survived – freedoms and liberties were steadily eroded "to increase public safety." Yeah, I remember that Hitler said the same thing about why he passed some of those laws he did too.

Throughout all of the situations, the politicians got on television and talked about remaining calm; being prepared; cooperating with the authorities. They were all very reassuring about how great the CDC and WHO were and how everything was totally under control. They were so full of crap.

But once the outbreak happened in Washington, DC – and other world capitals - those politicians were all of a sudden singing a different tune. Very quickly there was no "remain calm" or "cooperating with the authorities." The Capitol Building emptied out like a five-gallon bucket turned upside down with no lid – from the top of a tall building. All those elected officials were climbing over each other to get to their limousines, helicopters and planes. In what was one of the oddest happenings of all time, the Secret Service in conjunction with the Capitol Hill Police Department declared a state of emergency for the District of Columbia, and neither the city police department nor the mayor's office argued it for a single minute. I don't know who told who what, but the message was passed quick and clear: it's about to get ugly FAST. Do what we say or die with the rest.

I guess it was only reasonable that high density population centers saw the fastest spread of the virus. After all – one zombie in a corn field isn't as dangerous as one zombie on a subway train. All those cities – what became referred to as "NFL cities" in America (they all had pro football teams) – became explosive breeding grounds for the zombies.

All of the fictional stories you've seen about the societal collapse that occurs during a pandemic… they aren't fiction. Law enforcement was overwhelmed so fast that they literally had to fight to stay alive to get home – or even just out of the cities – at the end of their shift. The good news was that every cop had almost fifty rounds of ammunition on their gun belt. The bad news was that for every cop in a big city there's usually between 2,500 and 5,000 citizens if not more. There was just no way they could fight their way out when the zombie hoards started flooding out of apartment buildings, parks, business offices, hospitals, morgues and more.

I think the hardest part was watching an entire high school empty itself of zombies. The principal, meaning well I'm sure, had ordered a "lock down and shelter in place" when it seemed like things were getting too bad for the students to go outside. His rationale as he explained it in his memoirs was simple: there was food on hand for a week; a clean water supply; showers and a nurse (health care). It was a simple matter of waiting secure inside the school for the authorities to secure the city outside the school. Unfortunately for him and every other person in the school, some of the food had been contaminated somehow, and within a day over 200 students were dead. The next day there were 200 zombies hunting and feasting on the other 1,400 students, staff and faculty members. Three days after the first contaminated food was eaten, over 1,600 zombies broke out of the school.

That's something that the television shows, books, radios and more never really prepared us for. It's one thing to think about putting a high velocity chunk of lead through an adult zombie's cranial vault. It's something entirely different to point that gun at a kid who was 14, looked about 12, and was coming at you wanting to feast on your flesh. For some of us the choice wasn't all that hard and we got over it pretty quick. The others… well, we ended up having to ventilate their skulls too.

By the time the general population fully realized that a worldwide zombie pandemic was occurring, the zombies probably accounted for about 15% of the total population. The challenge we faced was this: their numbers grew geometrically. If we couldn't stop them in an equal fashion, the planet was doomed.

Just like a self-defense instructor teaches his (or her) students to never quit fighting, to overcome violence with greater violence, we realized that if we… if the world was to survive with humans as the dominant species, then we'd have to start "killing" zombies at a greatly increased rate. Imagination and creativity came into play. Safety concerns – at the level of airborne infectious diseases – were a major factor in our strategy.

Truth be told, killing them one on one is pretty easy. They aren't fast; they don't realize that their existence is about to come to and end, so they don't duck, seek cover or flinch. If you can hold your gun steady enough to pull the trigger on target, you can stop them as fast as you can acquire your target, steady the weapon and squeeze off the next round. If you don't have a gun, you can accomplish the same task by hitting them with a sharp cutting object such as an axe or sword, or you can beat their brains out (literally) with a good bat or other blunt weapon.

Two things I'll mention here that will get reinforced later in this story.

First, if you are hacking or hitting them, you need to insure that you don't get any of the gore on you. It's 100% infectious. The zombie virus – what is commonly referred to as Solanum since about 2010 – is carried in EVERY cell of a zombie's being. It doesn't matter what type of tissue it is; if it came off of or out of one of them and gets into your system, you're infected and your time is short.

Second, if you decapitate them, the head is still dangerous. To make a head no longer dangerous you have to destroy the jaw structure. The mouth and jawbone have to be so damaged as to not function sufficiently to bite. THEN the head is no longer a threat UNLESS you do something stupid that splatters bits of it all over you or someone else.

With all that out of the way, let me tell you this: it's amazing what you can get used to. It was almost three months after the acknowledged worldwide zombie outbreak pandemic before it really inconvenienced my life. Guns had always been a part of my day and I always had plenty of ammo. Hey, I'm a redneck – what do you expect? Knives, hatchets, tomahawks... they were nearly always within reach around the house in some form. I didn't live in a heavily populated area, and the folks around my area have a pretty high level of common sense – not like those nincompoops that live in the cities sucking their lattes and fighting over worthless paper money. Me and my neighbors grew our own food; hunted our own meat; fixed our own vehicles and looked out for each other. We were careful; courteous; respectful; thoughtful.

Then one day – like I said, about three months in – a car raced up around the others in line at one of the town's entry points. The city cops and deputies from the sheriff's office had set up roadblocks at every road in or out of town. Most were clean blocked, but at three of them were openings you could drive through after being checked out by the boys and girls wearing badges. Ours is a small town so it was rare that anyone's identity or health was questioned. Everybody knew everybody. Then some idiot from "the big city" decided he was going to zoom around everyone in line, crash his car into the guard shack, flip it over, blow it up and scatter his infected remains all over about two dozen people.

Of course we didn't know it at the time but those two dozen folks were the walking dead, unaware of what awaited them in the next 24 hours. By noon the next day, they'd all died. By noon the day after that, they were all biting, eating and infecting their family members. By noon the day after that, those of us who were armed and prepared were ventilating zombie skulls without pause, hesitation or remorse.

That was when I learned about two folks in the town I would forever be glad to call friend: Travis Anvil Stone – now a famous "zombie killer" – and Justin Rustovic – a Russian three generations into American citizenship. Apparently, well before anything got ugly, Stone had seen it coming and prepared himself. Rustovic, as I understand it, had seen the writing on the wall and had hired Stone to help train the Russian's family; all of them. Hell, even his twelve-year-old son can take out zombies with head shots from over 100 yards away.

I made it a point to introduce myself to them and offer to work in cooperation with them. It was a beneficial alliance. Justin and his family had a hard way to go of it, and this story is mostly about them. The parts in between – the lessons learned about planning and preparation – they all come from Travis A. Stone. I am thankful every day that what I learned from the both of them has kept my skin a healthy shade of pink instead of an ugly mottled shade of gray. Then again, if the day ever comes where I get infected, I know Stone and Rustovic: my skull will be ventilated about five seconds after infection so I'll never be a zombie… and I'm thankful for that.

3

CONTEMPORARY ZOMBIES

In the year 2011 a new report was released that indicated the "zombie culture" was a five billion dollar industry – and that was just in North America. As was mentioned early on in this book, part of the plethora of zombie-related material that was released was pushed out to make big governments happy. A lot of it, though, was produced simply because the topic became so popular. In late 2011 if you searched the popular online book/products store Amazon.com for the word zombie you'd get about 9,000 results. That's a lot of zombie reading. Ironically, the number one item returned in such a search was a book about surviving a zombie outbreak written by a gentleman named Max Brooks. Max was a foresight genius where zombies were concerned, and his books about them inspired huge growth in the simple interest that surrounded them.

But truth be told, zombies in literature started well before Max was ever born. In fact, if you look at what a zombie is and does

– the risen dead eating human flesh to stay animated (even though their digestive systems are completely dysfunctional) – you see where the same thing can apply to some fictional creatures. The big difference between zombies and those fictional creatures? The "fictional" part.

Take, for example, mummies. In one popular mummy movie of the late 20th century, the mummy was brought back from the dead, reanimated with magic, but then had to replace rotted away and deteriorated body parts, not to mention recollecting his organs that had been stored in ceramic jars for millennia. The mummy takes some body parts from humans and consumes the life force from other humans. Think about it...

Mummy takes body parts from humans.
Mummy consumes energy from humans.
Zombies consume human flesh.
Zombies eat body parts from humans.

Is it really so different in concept? Not so much...

And while fictional creatures like mummies (which are only fictional in the sense that they can't be reanimated as far as we know) are the walking undead, zombies are different in that they are only dead in certain ways. More on that later in the proper educational chapter.

Take a look around though. Walk through a bookstore. Search the word "zombie" online. Heck, search "zombie, CDC, pandemic" and see what you get back. Don't limit your thinking to that single word "zombie" though. Open your brain (before one of them does) and realize that the theme of raising the dead, the walking undead, etc., is nothing new. Heck, there are even Biblical stories about the dead being raised and brought back to life. While that's definitely not a zombie story, it IS an "animated dead" story, is it not? How long has this theme been a part of the human experience?

Research reveals that the *Epic of Gilgamesh*, a Mesopotamian work of literature comprised of legends and poems about the character Gilgamesh, written in about 700 B.C., referred to *"…the dead go up to eat the living! And the dead will outnumber the living!"*[7]

Given that we're now in the early part of the 21st century, unless my math is incorrect, we've held zombies – even if by another name – as part of the collective human psyche for about 2,800 years; almost three millennia. That is significant in and of itself.

In popular books – some of which have become movies – zombies have existed even if in a form that isn't common to society's acceptance of them today. Mary Shelley's *Frankenstein*, published in 1818, was about a reanimated body comprised of the parts of different corpses. Remember how the original Frankenstein was described as moving and walking? It's the same way he was depicted in the movie *Frankenstein* in 1931. He was gray/green and moaned. He walked in a stilted fashion with his arms upraised, pointed out in front of him as if reaching for a nonexistent support. If that doesn't sound like a modern day zombie as we know it, I don't know what would.

The actual word "zombie" was brought into mainstream entertainment by way of movies as early as the 1932 film *White Zombie* starring none other than the famous Bela Lugosi. How coincidental is it that *Frankenstein* – with a large, slow moving, arms out gray monster made from reanimated flesh – was released in 1931 and then the first movie with "zombie" in the name, *White Zombie*, was released just a year later?

In 1943 folks enjoyed the movie *I Walked With A Zombie*. That was the last film for a while that had the word zombie in the title. After that, the producers, writers, directors and such got a little more careful with their wording. One can't help but wonder why?

Then in 1954, author Richard Matheson wrote what, after *Frankenstein*, can probably be recorded as the first contemporary successful zombie-lore book: *I Am Legend*. From 1964 (*The Last Man On Earth*) to 1971 (*The Omega Man*) to 2007 (*I Am Legend*), the book was made into three different movies, all of them depicting a single human male left alone to survive in a world populated by undead bloodsucking/human flesh eating beings who used to be human. If you watch those movies and pay attention, you can learn some good lessons. It's almost as if the writer had foreknowledge, or first hand knowledge, of what a zombie pandemic would be like and how the zombies would behave.

In 1968 when George A. Romero made the movie *Night of the Living Dead* – the first modern day acknowledged zombie movie – he readily admitted the impact that *I Am Legend/ The Last Man On Earth* had on his development. For the first time that can be found on record, a movie depicted a zombie – the living dead – eating the flesh of a freshly killed and/or not quite dead human… **IN 1968!** Remembering that we have seen a measurable increase in the number of zombie outbreaks since 1848, is it any wonder that Hollywood finally caught up? It only took, after all, 120 years. Forty-four years later we've seen original movies, remakes of movies, sequels, prequels, books, graphic novels, video games and more all based on the zombie reality: Solanum isn't fake; the zombie threat isn't fiction.

So here we find ourselves in the early parts of the 21st century. About 15 years in to be exact. With all of today's technology, the Internet, bloggers, "news" reporters and more, how many zombie attacks do you think we can find documented since the turn of the century? Since "Y2K" shook everyone with fear in their boots?

NOT A SINGLE ONE.

Really? After averaging one every 4.7 years, we can't find a single documented zombie attack anywhere in the world in the past 13 years?

Nope. Why do you think that is?

Sit up and pay attention. Look around and recognize reality. Since October of 2001 there have been wars raging in various parts of Africa, South America and the Middle East. The wars in the Middle East are (allegedly) in direct response to terrorist attacks against the United States. Those same terrorist attacks were used to push through "The Patriot Act;" a piece of legislation that gives the federal government in the United States awesome power to control information, search people's private information, and reach into nearly any existent database to take out whatever they need to "investigate and prosecute terrorists." Do you really think that's all the governments of the world are doing?

With a little applied logic and some reasonable speculation, we can predict where some zombie outbreaks may have occurred. Think about the disasters that have happened since 2001.

In 2001 – 2002, wars in Afghanistan and Iraq with bleed over on occasion into Saudi Arabia, Pakistan and Kuwait. Anytime you have a large number of people injured or killed you have a chance of infections breaking out. Anywhere you see a viral infection spreading through an indigenous population with armed "outsiders" moving in for any purpose – and war is a nice generic one that world leaders can often leverage – then you have to wonder what else is going on.

In 2003, China lost over 2,100 citizens to "natural disasters" that are documented to have included flooding, "insect pest problems," earthquakes and droughts. Earthquakes are obvious and measurable. Droughts and flooding, though, can be sensationalized and leveraged easily. And really? "Insect pest problems?" Why didn't they just SAY "infectious deadly diseases spread by mosquitoes?" The Chinese government put a man from the State Environmental Protection Administration (China has an EPA?) in charge of the recovery and cleanup effort.

In 2004, nearly all of western Africa was reported to be suffering from a locust outbreak that resulted in response teams from no less than 20 countries being sent to fight the problem. Oddly, while pest control seemed to be a priority, all of the supplies and equipment shipped in could also be used for biological sterilization of a given area and to wipe clean infected areas. The pest control efforts, according to reports, spread from Mauritania on the west coast of Africa all the way to Egypt, Jordan and Israel. While the Desert Locust is obviously named for the locale in which it breeds, it still depends on food and would not migrate across vast expanses of barren earth. So what were those 20 multi-national teams actually chasing all the way across Africa?

In 2005, Hurricane Katrina swept through the Gulf of Mexico and tore into parts of Mississippi, Alabama and Louisiana – specifically New Orleans. While no one believes (yet) that any government can manipulate the weather to such an extreme, many people question the actions of responding governmental units after the fact. Where levees failed to hold back the Gulf and the Mississippi River, many reported that the U.S. Army Corps of Engineers had blown them up. The Federal Emergency Management Administration was reportedly slow in its response, but the Federal Environmental Protection Agency (EPA) seemed to be there almost before the hurricane hit. What was the EPA's primary goal? Based on their behavior, it was to contain all of the coffins and bodies that floated out of the above-ground crypts when the flood waters washed through.

It was reported that over 1,800 people were killed as a result of Hurricane Katrina, but a huge portion of those numbers are counted well after the hurricane had passed. In fact, with a little research, you'll see that the actual number of deaths that occurred DURING the hurricane is pretty small. Add to that the number of law enforcement officials who were literally begging for any cop in the country to come help, one of the largest activations of a private security force in history, and the fact that the political leaders were so afraid of the survivors' panic that they ordered the seizure of every privately owned firearm and you have to be left wondering: what really happened there?

In 2006 in Kampung Pasir, Malaysia, a landslide was reported. Immediately prior to the landslide it was reported that a village in the area had experienced an outbreak of an unidentified virus that was causing panic amongst the villagers. Reports included stories of infected people being hacked apart with machetes but that the dismembered parts were still "alive." Then a series of explosions was heard, the landslide occurred and the entire village was buried under what was estimated to be about sixty feet of mud and rock. There were no reported survivors.

In 2007, it looks like mankind got away with no suspicious activity that could have been an outbreak or a cover-up for one.

In 2008, there was another landslide in Malaysia, this time in Bukit Antarabangsa. It was the same story as in 2006. An epidemic level viral infection, explosions, landslides and buried village. No survivors.

In 2009, there were avalanches reported in a number of countries to include Afghanistan, El Salvador, Zigana and in the United Kingdom. Now, honestly, how often do you hear of an avalanche in the United Kingdom? In every case there were reports of sick citizens or villagers, explosions prior to the avalanches or landslides and zero survivors afterward. It seems that world governments have found an efficient way to cover up, literally, zombie outbreaks. Do you live at the bottom of a steep mountain side or potentially muddy hill?

In addition to these suspected zombie outbreaks in recent years, the "zombie" craze has been used by virtually hundreds of organizations to call attention to their cause. Political parties have used the zombie image to depict followers of other political ideologies. Nonprofit health research organizations have used the same image, colored or dressed a particular way, to call attention to their research efforts; leveraging zombie lovers to raise funds.

Obviously no one ever complains about such things (well, maybe they complain about the political junk). Using a popular topic within society to call attention to a cause or to raise funds for research to fight a debilitating disease just seems like a good marketing ploy.

Finally, we see that even the federal government used the zombie craze as a method of calling attention to the need to prepare. As the Centers for Disease Control wanted the American populace to make basic preparation in case of a biological weapons attack, and as much of the preparation is the same to defend against a zombie uprising, the CDC encouraged people to prepare for a zombie attack. The logic was sound: if people did half of what was suggested then they'd be better prepared in the event of an actual terrorist or nation-state attack committed on the United States using biological or infectious disease weapons.

Now, when the government starts using "the latest fad" to garner attention to a specific action, it's probably a good idea to pay attention. That means the government is near desperate, and indeed they were. Unbeknownst to most of us, the zombie outbreaks were obviously increasing and the government was trying to stem the tide… to no avail.

Take note of the timeline: prior to 2002 we were seeing average of one zombie outbreak every 4.7 years. SINCE 2002 we're averaging one per year OR MORE. Get the hint? The governments of the world realized that they clearly could not continue to efficiently contain the outbreaks. More importantly, they realized that they couldn't guarantee a quarantine on the information. Every world leader knew that once the zombie outbreak information was confirmed as fact instead of fiction, societies worldwide would start to fall apart. It would have been nice if they'd just given us a little warning. Instead, they left the average citizen to fend for himself and his family while the "elite" of the world put walls of humans between themselves and the hungry zombies. Ironically, the large majority of the world leaders fell victim to Solanum themselves within the first year or two of the larger outbreaks.

It should have been obvious to them that it would happen and why. Rich people – which all world leaders are, even if by their own local standards – are surrounded by other people. They have to have their entourage, servants, ego boosters, drivers, pilots, masseuses, etc. The more people you have around the greater the chances are that at least one of them is infected. When you have hundreds of people around, the chances increase that several of them are infected. Any time you have a zombie infection within a high-density residential population area the infection rates soar both in quantity and speed. Welcome to every city's nightmare and the new reality for every rich person who insists on being catered to.

4

HOW THE "ZOMBIE FAD" SLAPPED ME IN THE FACE

So, there I was minding my own business, surfing the Internet looking for some ballistic data tables when I came across a friend's website. This particular friend had served in the Navy as part of the Special Warfare Community (okay, okay: he'd been one of those famous or infamous Navy SEALs). While he was in the Navy he had been tasked with developing some no-light shipboard defense tactics. When he got out, he took those tactics and created a training program for delivery to police officers, security folks, etc. Needless to say, he was not the kind of guy who paid attention to unimportant fads.

Then, as I said, one day I landed on his website while I was searching for some ballistic data tables. He had what I was looking for in his resource section, but the information was accompanied by additional information on how different wavelengths of light could be used to identify zombies in low light conditions. Apparently, and I had never thought about it but it was obviously true, we see only in shades of gray if there's not enough light to discern colors. If the person you're aiming your gun at IS gray though, you'd better be sure of your shot placement. And if they AREN'T gray but LOOK gray because there's insufficient light to see how pink their skin is, then you DON'T want to take that shot. You see the conundrum.

Well my friend had developed a filter that fit onto the end of any standard "tactical" hand-held light. The filter changed white light sufficiently so that actual gray skin looked gray but every other shade of skin looked yellowish. If you attended his training program or read his literature you'd see that you could use the light filter to identify zombies even in a low light environment.

For a few moments I sat there thinking what a cool idea that was and how smart he was for leveraging the zombie fad. Then I realized that he wasn't the kind of guy who would waste his time on such stuff unless he saw a true and immediate need for such. In other words, HE believed that zombies were real and posed a serious threat that needed to be addressed.

The realization made me stop and think.

I fell asleep that night with the realization still on my mind. The next morning I started a new research project that would eventually change my world. I started searching for information about real historically documented zombie attacks. After filtering out everything I considered to be BS, I still had several dozen left.

Then I researched all of the various potential and alleged causes of zombieism from religion to drugs to mysticism to scientific or viral. I was surprised to find several medical periodicals that had published research papers from various doctors indicating that zombies were indeed real and that they were the result of either a viral infection or a drug-induced condition.

Finally I searched through reams of documents to see if I could find proof that governments were aware of an actual zombie epidemic or pandemic threat and, if so, what actions they had planned to deal with it. What I found was a direct result of the WikiLeaks scandal that occurred in 2010. Out of the hundreds of thousands of documents they had released, the ones the governments of the world seemed most concerned about resecuring or covering up all contained information about large scale responses to massive viral outbreaks. I'm not sure I'd have noticed except for the information contained about mass graves and the depth of a mix of dirt, mud and/or rock that was necessary to secure the bodies from "any potential scavenger that might release organic material." It seemed a pretty odd way to me to refer to bodies or scavengers that might dig up and drag out body parts. "...release organic material." It read as if they were more worried about containment than decent and proper burial or the rest of the souls of those who had died.

Further research into the referenced documents of THOSE documents showed that they all came from either the World Health Organizations, the American Medical Association, the United States Military's Special Operations Command (SOCOM) leadership or, although it was the least frequently referenced, the Centers for Disease Control (CDC).

I probably spent about three to four hours digesting everything I had found. I wasn't sure what my next step should be, but I WAS sure that something was going on and I needed to find a way to verify it, or at least get more evidence in support of my belief about what I'd discovered.

Since I'm a military veteran and I have plenty of friends who made a career of it, I made a few phone calls. I have one or two friends who are assigned within SOCOM, but I have a lot of friends who are still in and are in line combat units. The first call I made was to a friend at Ft. Bragg. He couldn't tell me anything about pandemic preparations, and he actually laughed when I brought up the topic of zombies. After he finished laughing though, he commented about how his most recent pistol qualifications had been done on what he had thought were joke targets. They were zombies, and the only qualifying shots were head shots.

Next I called a buddy in Little Creek, Virginia. He laughed even harder at the idea of zombies, reassured me that all their training and work was still geared toward anti-terrorism efforts… and then made the same observation about zombie targets used for handgun training.

My next call was to Ft. Benning where I got a Colonel friend of mine on the line. Our conversation was light and cheerful until I brought up the topic of pandemic infectious disease. All of a sudden his answers became short and there was no friendliness in his voice. When I joked about how tense the conversation had gotten and offered to lighten the moment, he said, "That would be good. Go ahead." So I mentioned a pandemic zombie outbreak… and he hung up on me.

My last phone call was to a friend who is in the Marine Corps Expeditionary Unit (MEUSOC). He refused to discuss with me, in any way on the phone, anything having to do with pandemic infectious diseases, and when I tried to joke about zombies he got silent. He refused to acknowledge anything I had said. His final words to me were, "Whenever I get home next, you and I can talk over beers, face to face, but that's the only way some things will ever get discussed." He never did get home; we never did get those beers; I found out after the fact that many units from SOCOM were put in front of the zombie nation to slow them down. It angered me because the SOCOM troops weren't used to save civilians or even infrastructure. They were sacrificed to save politicians and rich people.

So after those phone calls, I had what I felt was proof positive that our government, military commands, the CDC and the WHO all believed several things:

- ☣ That zombies were real;
- ☣ That the zombie "infection" could be easily spread;
- ☣ That military action would be required to contain it;
- ☣ That it presented a real and immediate threat.

My next steps were clear. I began my research on how to prepare to survive a zombie outbreak. In this case, I had to assume that I was looking at an imminent worldwide zombie pandemic that would destroy society's structure, disrupt virtually every supply line our civilization depended on, and would likely last for several months before it was either brought under control OR the zombies began to depopulate through the national order of their function. (More on that in the next chapter.)

I quickly realized that most of my preparations would be identical to what they would be in the event of a biological attack on our country either from another country or by terrorists. My food storage, water storage and house fortification would be about the same as well. While I was no stranger to weapons, I realized that I needed to upgrade my armory and increase my training because, as everyone knows (although most don't know WHY), only a head shot stops a zombie. Thankfully they usually move slowly enough that scoring head shots isn't that big of a deal.

As I began my preparations, I also continued my research. The biggest chore, quite honestly, was sorting all the BS from the valid information. I quickly realized that everyone who had ever watched a zombie movie, mummy movie, or any other horror movie, as well as anyone who had ever played one of a handful of video games, automatically assumed they were an "expert" on zombie fighting. What a joke.

Of course, not everything happens in a single day, and it was about a week later that I was in my local big chain superstore stocking up on some more .45ACP ammunition when I heard screams coming from the front of the store. Being the curious kind of person that I am, I headed that way to see what was going on – and to determine whether I could help, be a good witness, or escape out a back fire door. None of those three options appeared correct when I saw a person - well, a thing really – chewing on a woman's shoulder.

As I watched, the woman broke loose and ran away, blood streaming down her body front and back. Subconsciously I registered the fact that she likely had an arterial injury and she'd bleed to death pretty quick if she didn't get the necessary medical attention. I wasn't prepared to provide it though, and my attention was taken away from her when another scream pierced the air. As slow as the zombie was moving, he was able to grab another person – this one looking to be an adolescent male – and bite into him.

My first thought was, "How can you stand around completely unaware of what's going on around you in a public place?" My next thoughts registered the kid's ear buds indicating that he was listening to music and likely didn't even hear the previous screams. His mother, on the other hand, looked like she was in shock and incapable of a coherent thought.

Customers were streaming out the front doors of the store, some of them without paying for their purchases, and pandemonium reigned. I didn't perceive a threat at that moment and I knew the deputies would be on their way, so I positioned myself with plenty of obstacles between myself and the zombie and watched what would happen.

As a side note, it's important to mention that the zombie didn't look horror-movie-rotted-flesh ugly. He must have been a relatively fresh zombie because his skin had just started to gray, almost as if he'd been sick for several days, and he wasn't reeking or overly dirty yet. In fact, if he hadn't been attacking people, he'd look like many other department store customers, which was probably how he managed to get so far into the store unnoticed before his hunger drove him to attack.

Back to the incident: the teenager finally broke away from the thing after a brief struggle, punched it hard in the face – which had absolutely zero effect – and then ran for the front door, one hand covering the bleeding injury caused by the zombie's bite. I could hear sirens getting closer outside and continued to watch as the zombie looked around.

It struck me that every zombie movie I'd ever seen showed zombies as mindless, directionless, moving as if on autopilot and encountering victims by accident or coincidence. Watching this zombie actually turn its head seeking to find the next person to bite was chilling; it was a reality check.

I'll give the security guard credit. She came right over, nightstick in hand, and delivered a solid hit to the thing's shoulder blades. I knew why she hadn't hit it in the head: that's a potential lethal force attack. It wasn't justified right at that moment. That said, the hit across its shoulder blades had as much effect as the teenager's punch to the face had: zero. She tried again to no avail, but she did manage to get its attention. As it turned on her, she caught up with the program and swung for left field, hitting it just under its jaw line. I thought she was going to knock its head off its body as hard as she hit it.

The thing's head tilted over some just from the force of the impact, but the hit otherwise had no effect. The zombie stepped toward her; she stepped back and swung again. Another solid hit. More zero effect. The zombie stepped toward her, its arms coming up as if to reach for her. She stepped back and swung again – this time with both arms holding her end of the nightstick.

I saw the zombie's skull cave in as the stick made impact just above its left ear. The zombie staggered and moved toward her another half step. She cocked back for another swing.

At that moment the first deputy came through the front doors. The zombie registered another uniform presence. Don't ask me why. The deputy was big. Maybe he presented a more tasty potential food source? Seeing what was going on, the deputy pulled out his nightstick. Where the security guard's was wooden or plastic/polymer, the deputy's was a collapsible steel shaft, a "friction lock baton" made by ASP. He drew it, extended it and swung it on the move.

Just as the security guard's stick hit the zombie on the left side of the head again, the deputy's baton hit the thing full on horizontally across the forehead. Between the two strikes, the skull structure was severely damaged, and I thought the top of the thing's head was going to come off completely. As it was, the zombie staggered again, tried to take another step and got hit twice more.

This time the top of its head pretty much did come off. Brains spilled out looking like pudding, and the body slowly began to sag. For having had its brains bashed in – or out, I guess I should say – the thing took a long time to actually collapse to the floor. It staggered, dropped to its knees, began to bend at the waist and finally crumpled to end up in a heap of yuck.

The deputy was talking on his radio, saying something about a biohazard situation and ordering a containment of the area while requesting members from the county's Hazardous Materials (HAZMAT) team to come in. Part of me was a bit miffed. I was going to be stuck there until someone cleared me to leave. On the other hand, I'd be able to see a lot more and get more information. I wasn't sure what the deputy did or didn't know, but the security guard looked entirely clueless. She was babbling about the need to call an ambulance "for the suspect." The deputy was trying to hush her up. If there hadn't been a zombie leaking brains on the floor, it would have been almost humorous.

The next two deputies who arrived were dressed in OD Green uniforms which I knew made them members of the county's SWAT team. Both had on heavy-duty rubber gloves, sealed with rubber bands around their forearms, and protective masks. The masks weren't the old military surplus M-17 or M17A1 gas masks but looked like brand new models from a company called Draeger. The same company made rebreathers for the Navy's special warfare guys, and I knew they were making protective masks. I didn't realize that the masks were already in use.

Those deputies immediately disabled the electric motors that opened and closed the automatic front doors, and then they had the doors locked. People who wanted to leave were being told that they might have been exposed to a virus and that they couldn't leave until a hazardous materials team doctor cleared them. Some were upset. One tried to push his way past the deputies. He ended up, rather quickly, face down and handcuffed. It served as an object lesson for the rest.

It was hours later before I was cleared and allowed to leave. I had been tested for any viral contamination by way of mouth swabs, urine testing and blood testing. They had swabbed the inside of my cheeks twice, had me pee in a cup (and had DEMANDED at least four ounces which seemed odd) and had pricked my finger to get a few drops of blood. When I was cleared and allowed to leave the building, I was stopped before being allowed to leave the parking lot. Two detectives – one county and one state – took all of my identifying information, had me fill out a medical questionnaire and then asked me a bunch of questions about what had happened inside.

On the one hand, I felt pretty complimented because they seemed delighted with the detail of events that I could provide. On the other hand, it was creepy because they seemed more interested in how much gore splatter there was from the zombie (not that they called it that) than they were about whether or not the use of force was justified. I was finally released about seven hours after the incident had occurred. I was told not to leave the state until I had heard back from the local HazMat team leader about further test results.

Everything I had seen, especially after all the information I had previously gathered, confirmed for me that our nation – and possibly the world – was experiencing a far-reaching zombie outbreak. Only an idiot wouldn't prepare properly. The first thing I did when I got home was load all my guns, place them strategically around my home, and begin taping heavy plastic over the windows. My neighbors – the ones who saw me through the windows – looked at me like I was half crazy… but that really wasn't anything new.

5

RECOGNIZING THE THREAT

As was discussed in earlier chapters, many different causes of zombieism have been documented and theorized. In reality, the term "zombie" is used to describe not only those who have died and been reanimated, but also those who have their state of consciousness altered by pharmacology and/or those who simply allow their brains to run on "low power" to the point of seeming slow, out of touch, brainless or brain dead.

The loose use of the term "zombie" to describe those who are voluntarily – and sometimes aggressively – brain dead shouldn't be dismissed. While these people aren't infected and don't pose a physical threat, they do pose a long-term threat to society's security and stability. By voluntarily not exercising their brain power; by voluntarily keeping themselves ill- or uninformed; by ignoring the world around them, these voluntarily brain-dead "zombies" will eventually grow to become either nonproductive members of society or parasites on the skin of society. As such, they present almost as large of a threat as actual infected zombies do. Neither of them does society any good; one is just actively more dangerous than the other. Of course, Darwinism works, and the voluntarily brain dead often and easily become prey to the true zombie.

Obviously you have nothing to fear from the mindless nitwit who drools in front of television all day or who sits around in public with his mouth hanging open looking like he wants to catch flies. While these people are a long-term threat to society as a whole, they present no physical threat to individuals unless they assume this mindless state while operating machinery.

Now, let's look at the pharmacological zombie. In 1985, a gentleman named Wade Davis published a book titled *The Serpent and the Rainbow*. In 1988, Mr. Davis published a second book titled *Passage of Darkness: The Ethnobiology of the Haitian Zombie*. After having traveled to Haiti to complete his research, Mr. Davis published his works detailing how he believed a person could be "zombiefied" by the administration of two drugs into their system. Mr. Davis contends that the mix of the neurotoxin Tetrodotoxin and the dissociative drug Datura together would render a normal person into a near-death state. He further contends that the drugs would also make the person almost 100% subjective to external control.

It is no big surprise that Mr. Davis' work has been argued against vehemently. Educated people including doctors, scientists, psychologists and psychiatrists have all argued that the administration of Tetrodotoxin alone is usually fatal and that the addition of drugs such as Datura would not create a near-death but alive individual who could walk around and function, especially not in the manner most people assume zombies will move, i.e., slow speed, arms raised, glassy (or milky) eyed, moaning and (sometimes) drooling.

For all practical purposes, if a pharmacological zombie CAN be created, they are just as dangerous as a true zombie. They will perform whatever action their controller orders them to, and they will not hesitate to kill in whatever manner they can accomplish. Given their potentially slow movements and detached mannerisms, it is likely that once they finally get hold of their intended victim, the most likely weapon they will use is their teeth, fingernails and hands. The wounds that would be caused are, for all intents and purposes, just as horrific as those caused by true zombies except that the victim will only die once and not be reanimated. With that in mind, if you HAVE to be killed by a zombie, it's far better to be killed by one created pharmacologically. That said, defending yourself against any zombie requires the same tactics and strategies as discussed farther on.

The third and only real zombie is created by an infection of a virus. While some believe that Solanum is the cause, many others debate it. The scientific community by and large does not agree on the cause of zombieism but does agree that it is infectious and that the virus causing it is carried not only at the cellular level but in virtually every cell of an infected person's body.

Whatever the viral cause is, the existence of zombies – as noted in earlier chapters – is not open to debate. Their actions and activities across the millennia has been documented, and other evidence clearly suggests that their number and activities are accelerating.

To establish whether or not a zombie before you is a true zombie or a pharmacological zombie requires high levels of safety precautions as well as a laboratory equipped to do the necessary forensic analysis.

First the zombie must be captured. To avoid infection during said capture, if it's a true zombie, those attempting the capture must be fully protected in level 4 biohazard protection suits. This means an entirely sealed system with an internal air supply, sealed helmet, and an air/fluid proof suit that covers every part of the person's body. Once properly dressed, the capture team must overpower the zombie. While this isn't always difficult, it's both disgusting and potentially dangerous.

Since it's impossible for two items to come into contact without some matter transference occurring, it's obviously impossible for one person to grab another person without cells/matter being transferred. As the capture team contacts the zombie, infected zombie cells are shed onto the exterior of the biohazard suits. Because of this, and because temperature extremes in excess of 1000°F are the only way thought to destroy the zombie virus, the biohazard suits are considered "single use" items and have to be destroyed immediately following use.

Restraining the zombie once it's been overpowered is another challenge. Since they don't feel any pain, if you only strap them down at ankles and wrists, they will eventually pull their arm or leg free by pulling so hard against the restraint that they rip off the foot or hand holding them down. To avoid this occurrence, a zombie must be restrained in the following manner:

- ☣ On a solid backboard or gurney;
- ☣ Head strapped down – webbing across forehead;
- ☣ Neck strapped down – webbing across neck;
- ☣ Chest strapped down – webbing across chest above nipples;
- ☣ Biceps strapped down – webbing around/across biceps;
- ☣ Forearms strapped down – webbing around/ across forearms;
- ☣ Wrists strapped down – webbing around/across wrists;
- ☣ Waist strapped down – nylon webbing specified around waist;
- ☣ Thighs strapped down – webbing around/across thighs;
- ☣ Calves strapped down – webbing around/across calves;
- ☣ Ankles strapped down – webbing around/across ankles.

Only in this manner can the zombie be secured sufficiently to keep it from ripping its own extremities off to either escape or attack. Once strapped down in this fashion, further precautions must be taken to prevent the zombie from trying to bite medical workers and to keep the zombie from scratching the medical workers with its toenails or fingernails. To protect against bites, a large ball must be pushed into the zombie's mouth (racquetballs have been found to work well because they are hard enough not to be easily bitten but small enough to fit into most zombie's mouths) and then strapped or taped into place. To keep the hands and feet from trying to cause an injury to medical workers, they must be wrapped. Any cloth thick enough that they can't scratch through will suffice, but it must be applied in multiple layers and securely taped or tied into place.

With all of that accomplished, the medical/forensic team can begin its examination. Usually drawing blood is their first step and a clear indicator of what they're dealing with. A true zombie's blood is milky white (no red blood cells left) and thicker than normal human blood. A pharmacological zombie will still have normal-appearing blood which can be analyzed to determine what drugs are present in the system, if any.

If the blood is milky white and the team knows that it's dealing with a true zombie, other tissue samples can be taken from the large muscle groups, large organs, eyes, tongue and gums for analysis. The length of infection can be determined based on the destruction of the cell structure in the muscle tissue and the density of infected cells in the eyes and large organs.

Of course, such analysis is unnecessary if the zombie has been infected for more than 36-48 hours. In that time frame the skin becomes ashen and the zombie's body fat begins to burn off at an accelerated rate.

Whatever the zombie virus is, the infection proceeds along a clearly defined course of invasion, effect and outcome.

Having penetrated the body (see below for the ways that can happen), the virus reproduces by attaching to the red blood cells which carry it through the body's systems while it reproduces. At every organ, in every muscle, even inside the bone marrow, the virus is delivered as fast as it can reproduce. Rough estimates indicate that the virus takes approximately 18-24 hours to completely invade every organ, muscle and bone.

Throughout that time frame, the virus that has been delivered to the brain measurably increases its reproduction rate so that by the time the rest of the body has seen general infection the brain is 100% infected. That is to say that each and every brain cell, to include the entire medulla oblongata and the spinal cord, is infected with at least one virus cell.

The end result is that in approximately 24-28 hours, the person's body appears dead. The major organs cease to function; pulmonary and respiratory functions cease. It is important to note, however, that all of the zombie's senses still function, albeit in a slightly reduced fashion. The eyesight becomes hindered by the lack of fluid retention within the corneal structure. The olfactory senses work but are dependent on wind and breeze to carry scent through the nasal passages. Their sense of touch also has been proven to still exist, although their sense of pain seems to stop with their "death." Studies of incapacitated zombies have revealed that the virus infects the brain most heavily in the pain receptors, seemingly blocking any pain messages from getting through. So while the zombie feels pain, it doesn't perceive pain. It simply experiences more sensory input that it reacts to. The zombie's hearing obviously works, as they've been observed to change their direction of travel to pursue noises caused by healthy humans and large mammals. Finally, while we don't know if their taste buds function, it has been observed in a laboratory setting that their salivation glands still function but only in response to fresh mammalian blood.

Scientists have determined that the virus essentially changes the brain into a more powerful battery, increasing the power of the electromagnetic impulses it sends out to the muscles. The muscles continue to function in obedience to the brain until all fat has been burned off the body and the muscle has cannibalized itself beyond the ability to contract. Even though the zombie is "dead," the muscles still require fuel to function, and, just like starving people or those suffering from severe malnutrition, the body will consume itself. The zombie will eventually reach a state where it doesn't have enough fuel within itself to keep the muscles working and it will collapse. The brain will continue to fire out orders/electromagnetic impulses, but the muscles won't have any energy with which to comply.

What is left is a slowly rotting grayish body *that is still highly infectious and dangerous.* Until the body has been destroyed, *every cell still carries the virus and can invade the body of a healthy host*.

An interesting note that the scientists have discovered is the zombie virus cannot infect smaller mammals or any amphibian or reptile. The size limit seems weight related, and it's been determined that the zombie virus, in general, requires a mammal that is at least 90 pounds in size. That is a general number, and there have been documented cases of the zombie infection in mammals as small as 55 pounds. More important than the size or weight of the animal is the actual size of the brain. With an adult human brain weighing (on average) approximately three pounds[8], it was once thought that at least that size was required. It was later discovered that ANY mammal with a brain size of approximately 1.5 pounds or greater could be infected and converted.

Keeping that in mind, it's easy to understand why some dogs, such as German Shepherds and Golden Retrievers CAN become infected, while others, such as Dachshunds and Beagles can't be. It's a matter of the size of their brain. Smaller mammals such as squirrels and raccoons cannot be infected but, at least theoretically, porpoises and whales could be.

Something else that has been learned and is exceptionally important to know if you plan to survive a zombie uprising is how the zombie virus (Solanum if you believe that) can invade a human body and begin its infection of the systems. Thanks to mainstream popular movies and various books, many people believe that the only way to become a zombie is to be bitten by one. Since several movies also portray zombies as cannibalistic or, at best, surviving on the consumption of human brains, the zombie bite is usually the first step toward their "food intake." Obviously the victim then dies and is later reanimated as a zombie itself. (No one has ever been able to explain why, if a zombie needs to eat human flesh or brains, that the dead victims aren't consumed entirely. Why is there always enough left to become reanimated and functional? Oh, yeah – that's fiction!)

That the bite of a zombie can deliver the virus into a healthy human host is without question; however, that is far from the only method the virus can be spread. It is important at this juncture to share, and strongly encourage you to remember, a basic rule of forensic science:

> *Any time two objects come into physical contact*
> *with each other, an exchange is made and*
> *each is changed in some measurable way.*

Think about that carefully and understand the implications. Add onto that what was said earlier: EVERY cell in a zombie body carries the virus. The virus affects a human body at the cellular level. Every part of the human body is comprised of cells of various types.

THEREFORE, if a zombie scratches a human and even so much as a single cell of the zombie's fingernails or skin are delivered into the healthy humans skin, the infection has occurred. If a zombie's drool somehow ends up in a healthy human's mouth or even in an open cut or wound, then the infection has occurred. If pulverized zombie meat is sprayed around a given area because the zombie has been run over by a tractor trailer traveling at high speed, every piece of that zombie meat carries the virus and can spread the infection.

It took the scientists longer to figure this out than it did for active zombie hunters, like Travis A. Stone (see the foreword). Stone ascertained, upon seeing one of his hunting buddies infected by zombie back-splatter caused by a shotgun blast at close range, that the virus could be spread and the infection caused by other means than a bite. In fact, Stone was the first zombie hunter to begin mandating, at a minimum, respiration filters and wrap-around eye protection for all of his hunters. Any hunter who had an open wound had to clean it, bandage it, and tape securely over it with duct tape to insure no intrusion of the virus should contact occur with any zombie cells during a hunt.

With all that "scientific" information gleaned, the most basic questions were still the ones that mattered.

- ☣ What was the most effective and immediate way to stop a zombie?
- ☣ What precautions had to be taken if you were on the hunt?
- ☣ What decontamination procedures did you need to use after a successful hunt?

Since the zombie brain is the big battery that runs the zombie body, the most immediate way to shut a zombie's function down is to either destroy a significant portion of the brain OR separate the brain from the body. All those old movies that showed zombies being stopped by head shots delivered from guns were almost right. The key is to make sure that the gun you shoot it in the head with is of large enough caliber that the brain is sufficiently destroyed. The scientists think that destruction of 50% of the brain is sufficient because past that you have less than the required (approximate) 1.5 pounds of brain battery left to power the zombie. Many small-caliber guns simply don't do enough damage to shut a zombie down. As effective as a .22 Magnum round to the head might be in killing a live healthy human, it doesn't usually destroy enough zombie brain to cause shutdown.

For handguns, at a minimum, the following calibers are recommended:

- ☣ .38 Special (if fired within close range – 15 feet or less)
- ☣ .357 Magnum
- ☣ .357 Sig
- ☣ 9mm (see warning about .38 Special)
- ☣ .40 Smith & Wesson
- ☣ 10mm
- ☣ .41 Magnum
- ☣ .44 Special
- ☣ .44 Magnum
- ☣ .45 Long Colt
- ☣ .45ACP
- ☣ .45 GAP

All smaller calibers are considered ineffective, and even the calibers listed have very limited effective ranges to deliver sufficient damage as to reliably stop a zombie. Seven to ten yards should be considered the maximum range of use for handguns (with the possible exception of the .41 and .44 Magnum. You can stretch those engagement distances out to as much as 25 yards.)

For rifles, it's recommended that you avoid any caliber smaller than .30 and any round that travels slower than 2,500 feet per second (fps) coming out of the barrel. As a general rule of thumb, any round used by the police or military as a "sniper" round should be sufficient. Those would include (across the decades):

- ☣ .308
- ☣ .30-06
- ☣ .30-.30
- ☣ .444 Marlin
- ☣ .50 BMG

The 7mm Magnum *may* be used if shot placement is exceptional and complete separation of the brain from the spinal column is insured. The key word there is *complete*.

In the case of any zombie that is stopped with a gun shot to the head, only two things will actually shut the zombie down:

1) Destruction (or explosive removal) of 50% or more of the existing brain tissue, and/or

2) Complete separation of the existing/remaining brain tissue from the spinal column.

Now, since we've identified the stopping possibility of separating the brain from the spinal column, it becomes obvious that decapitating a zombie will also cause bodily shutdown; however, it's important to note that the head is still "alive" and presents a danger. ***The brain must still be destroyed.***

Once a zombie has been "shut down" by brain destruction, or if you come across one that has simply burned up its own muscle mass to the point of being inactive, proper disposal is required. A great number of labor hours were used by various world governments to gather and destroy zombie corpses.

Again, we have to thank Travis Stone. He was the first to suggest that if the bodies were left to rot where they fell (due to muscle burnout or effective zombie hunters), then the tissue could become airborne and/or be carried by scavengers. Both situations caused potential for the virus to be spread, so it became clear that zombie corpse disposal had to be prioritized.

To date, only two reliable methods have been identified for proper and complete disposal of a zombie corpse:

- ☣ Cremation
- ☣ Chemical acid destruction (chemical melting)

If the zombie corpse is cremated, the crematorium must reach a temperature of 800°F for the virus to be killed along with the cellular structure of the zombie. All bone fragments have to be reburned until only pure ash remains.

If the zombie corpse is chemically melted/destroyed, the melted biomass must be treated as a biohazard material and stored in an air-tight container, preferably underground, and the site protected against invasion. Although several world governments chose to use this method (ostensibly because they had huge stockpiles of various acids to be used as weapons of war), there was an obvious "chink in the armor:" earthquakes are entirely unpredictable, and if one caused a breach in the security of an underground zombie biomass storage site, then the potential for a large-scale virus exposure existed.

Finally, the CDC and WHO both released documents, after the largest zombie pandemic was under control and the actual number of zombies was being reduced that revealed all of the infectious diseases a zombie corpse could still carry and spread. They included virtually every viral strain of:

- Ebola
- Influenza
- Avian influenza (bird flu)
- Porcine influenza (swine flu)
- HIV
- HPV
- And virtually every other sexually transmitted disease that has ever been documented.

Additionally zombie corpses have also been found with live strains of:

- Measles
- Mumps
- Polio
- Bubonic plague
- And other diseases often thought almost totally eradicated via vaccine.

6

EXPERIENCE TEACHES
HARD LESSONS

As dictated by Justin Rustovic and notated by Frank Borelli.

My name is Justin Rustovic. As odd as it may seem, most of my family calls me "Just" and most of my friends call me "Russ." One man, Travis A. Stone, has always called me Justin, and he's about the only person in my life who has ever called me by my whole first name. Even my family called me "Russ" when I was growing up.

I'm a third generation Russian-American. My grandfather came to America right before the Second World War, and my father was born shortly thereafter. He and my mom were married young and had five kids: me, my two brothers and two sisters. I'm the middle child of the bunch. Before he died, my father made several good business investments, and, as a result, my siblings and I all became multi-millionaires when my father died. My mother didn't get any money in the will; just the house and whatever money she already had. It was apparently plenty.

Right after the turn of the century – and everyone's seemingly startled realization that the "Y2K" problem wasn't a problem – I did some research and came to believe that zombies were not fictional and that a pandemic was in the making. It took me some months before I shared my belief with anyone. At first I shared it with one of my older brothers; he laughed at me and dismissed what I said. Then I shared it with my wife; she laughed at me, then apologized for laughing and then refused to discuss the topic again.

In spite of people thinking I was silly or making fun of me, I continued to make my preparations for disaster. I stopped being specific about what kind of disaster I was preparing for, and my wife eventually got on board with the idea of being prepared. After all, natural disasters occurred all the time, and even power outages for just a day or two or three could be major inconveniences. So, just for the sake of common sense, she agreed that we should make some basic preparations.

After the Federal Emergency Management Agency (FEMA) came out with their recommendations for preparation, my wife got even more on board with the idea of preparedness. Without her knowledge, I continued to do my research into zombie pandemics/outbreaks, and it led me to a man named Travis Anvil Stone.

I had reached the point where I didn't think I could get any more prepared without more formal training, and everything I read said that Travis Stone was the man to help me out. So one night when my wife thought I was out watching a football game with some friends at the local sports bar, I sought out Travis. I knew he was in the nearby city for some consulting work and had a clue where he was staying. I checked out some of the area around his hotel and actually saw him in a back alley...

I couldn't believe my eyes at first. The drunk who had approached him looked kind of funny, but I hadn't identified it as a zombie. Stone apparently had. The gunshot was silenced, but the brain and gore spray was easy to see.

At first I was shocked. I mean, how often is it that you see one man stagger toward another and the second pull out a gun, level it at the first guy's head and squeeze off two quick shots? The only noise was the sound of the slide working on Travis' gun; that and the splatter of the zombie's brain and other matter against the wall.

I was standing half in the shadows and didn't move lest I be seen. I watched as the zombie fell, Travis holstered his gun and turned to leave the other end of the alley. Going back the way I had come, I went into the first bar I came to, and sure enough Travis had come in through the back and was sitting at the bar.

He looked at me carefully as I sat down next to him. The bartender walked over. I ordered a beer and thought about ordering Travis another round of whatever was already in front of him. Not yet, I thought to myself. My beer came and I took the first sip. The mug was chilled, and it made the beer seem all the more crisp.

"I saw what you did," I said in a quiet voice to Travis – but without looking at him. He was the only person close enough to hear me say it.

Out of the corner of my eye I saw him turn his head to look at me and I could feel the weight of his gaze on me. "Saw what?" he asked in his gravely voice.

I took another sip of beer, licked the foam off my lip and then replied. "I saw you take out that zombie." My voice was still quiet enough that no one else could hear. I turned to look at him to see what his reaction was. The bar hummed on around us, completely unaware that we were discussing a death... or a destruction, depending on how you looked at it.

The look on his face was cold. I couldn't tell if he was angry or simply didn't care about my existence.

"And?" he asked without any expression in his voice. "What's that mean to me?"

"Nothing," I said as carefully as I could. "I don't care beyond the fact that it proves I was right in what I came into the city for."

"And what was that?" he asked.

"To find you," I replied. I took another sip of beer.

"Why would you want to find me?"

I realized that he hadn't taken another swallow of his drink since I'd sat down. I wondered if he would. I took another sip of my nice cold beer in its chilled mug before answering him. Then I turned on my stool to face him, the side effect of which was to reduce the amount of distance between us. I wanted to be even quieter about what I said next.

"I want you to train me and my family," I said evenly. "No one else in the world is better at hunting and eradicating zombies, and I want my family to be trained."

He looked at me like he had a microscope between his face and mine. He was examining me. He was looking for any hint of joke or humor. I kept my face as hard as his was. No humor. No care. No concern. Just total coldness.

"Why would I do that?" he finally asked.

"Because we can help you. I have financial resources that comes from family. I am already prepared for natural disasters and many terrorist events. I'm not sure how much of it will apply to a zombie pandemic, but I want my family prepared. And right now they simply aren't."

He looked at me hard for another minute… and then another one. I held his stare and tried not to blink. This wasn't a game. I was dead serious, and I knew he was too. Finally he said, "Okay. We start now." Then he turned up his drink, swallowing whatever it was in three gulps. I downed the rest of my beer and promised myself I wouldn't have another one until I felt my family was ready for what was coming. We left the bar together and he followed me home.

My house is fair sized, and we have a detached four-car garage with an apartment over it. Travis moved into the apartment that night. My wife was pretty upset that I had a total stranger moving onto the property, and it took me several hours to calm her down. My children all seemed indifferent. Their outlook was that if I trusted Travis then he must be okay. My wife wasn't of that same opinion. She went to bed angry with me and got up to me fixing her breakfast. With her breakfast she read some of the articles I'd printed out from the Internet. Every one of them was about Travis Stone – noted zombie hunter.

The next few hours were strained to say the least. She didn't want Travis around. She thought I was wasting money. She thought I was delusional. She thought zombies were pure fiction and I was buying into a hyped up fad. She thought a lot... but not very much of me apparently.

What it boiled down to, about lunch time – and thankfully the kids were in school – was that I had committed myself and the family to learning from Travis. If she didn't agree with that, she was welcome to pack up and move out. The next two hours were the quietest my house had ever seen. Finally, just before the oldest child got home from school, she came to me and agreed. She also warned me that there was a limit to how much money she'd allow me to waste on this "fad" as she called it.

That evening Travis joined us for dinner and everyone got to ask him a few questions. By the time we'd gotten to dessert everyone in my family seemed to think Travis walked on water – or the next thing to it. From that point on we had evening "classes" on how to identify zombies, how the virus could spread, what we needed to do to prep the house, etc. On weekends we learned about weapons: guns, knives, impact weapons (that's what Travis called them), protective equipment such as gas masks, wrap-around ballistic eyewear and more.

That was our life for about a year. When almost exactly twelve months had passed, two things happened in the same day:

First, my wife told me Travis had to go. We'd spent a year learning everything he was willing to teach. We'd spent a small fortune preparing our house to defend against zombies and to make it "zombie proof." In her words, we'd embarrassed ourselves in front of our family and friends and she'd been tolerant long enough. We were either prepared or we weren't, but, either way, in her opinion, we were done with Travis Stone.

Second, Travis came and said he'd taught us all he could and it was time to move on. I was silently thankful for that. I wasn't sure how to tell the kids I was divorcing their mother, and Travis' statement saved me from having to.

I continued to read stories about Travis' adventures around the globe. Mysterious events continued to occur. I saw them all as zombie outbreaks that were covered up. My wife saw me as delusional still. The kids thought it was "cool" that dad was so into zombies, and they made fun of me because I didn't believe in zombie quite the way they were portrayed in the popular media blitz.

Three years passed…

And then there was a story about a homicide at the local department store. We live in a pretty well built up area –

although it's an hour's drive from the nearest big city. We have our share of major-chain department stores, restaurants, etc. At one of the department stores there were reports of a "zombie" – although the papers used the term as a joke based on the man's behavior – having attacked several people. As it was reported, the store's security guard had hit the thing pretty well several times with no effect. It took hits from both the security guard AND the first responding deputy to take the thing down. After that the scene was treated like a biohazard contaminated area.

I showed the reports to my wife and we discussed – in a totally rational manner (much to my surprise) – the chances that it was actually a zombie attack. We agreed to raise our level of awareness and institute a few of our basic home-zombie-proofing measures. We further agreed that three days should be more than enough to determine whether or not the attack at the department store had been a zombie attack and whether or not it would start an outbreak. After all, no one really knew for sure what kind of contamination had been spread.

Two days later the reports started coming in. Our little part of the world was seeing a zombie outbreak of significant proportions. Apparently, several dozen people in the department store had been infected by splattered gore and it had taken them this long to die (be transformed into a zombie), reanimate and then go out on the attack.

Thankfully – as odd as it sounds to say – all of them completed their change in their homes, so the largest number of casualties were their own families. Several of the smaller children were simply killed as the new zombies bit them, chewed on them, and essentially bled them dry. The older, larger, family members survived the bites only to fall prey to the infection, die, reanimate and come "alive" again as zombies themselves. As a result, it wasn't ONE zombie walking out of a house to go on the hunt. It was several zombies per household.

Do the math: Several dozen (so assume between two and three dozen or about thirty people total) were infected at the department store. They went home to their families; their husband or wife, and any children they had, and, in some cases, the family pets. One family had seven dogs, all of them big breeds, in addition to the five adolescent or young adult age children. That household alone turned out a total of seven zombie "people" and seven zombie dogs. One infected and dangerous zombie became fourteen in about 36-48 hours.

The smallest infected household only had the husband, the wife and one child. The child was a big ten year old; big enough to be infected and change. Three of them walked out of that house. It was later discovered that with an average of four zombies per household, and thirty of them originally, nearly 130 zombies actually wandered out on the hunt two days after the attack at the department store.

As soon as the first reports came in, my wife and I instituted ALL of our zombie preparations. Every member of my household put on a handgun – of 9mm caliber or larger – and every one of us took a long gun with us if we had to go outside for anything. IF we went outside at all we wore full coverage clothing including gloves taped at the wrists to our long-sleeve shirts, breathing masks and full wrap-around eye protection.

The biggest reason we went outside was to close and lock all the shutters that covered our windows. While most houses have ornamental shutters, we'd replaced ours with solid oak, two-inch thick hinged shutters. They closed from the outside but locked from the inside. After closing all the shutters, we poured bleach around the perimeter of our property and then again around the perimeter of the house. We turned off our air-conditioning and heating system and covered the outside air-handling units with heavy-duty construction trash bags, doubling them up and taping them into place with several wraps of duct tape.

Our neighbors laughed at us. We took it in stride. That night we heard the screams coming from a couple houses in the area. The zombies had found a way in… they were feasting. It meant more zombies would be out and about the next day. We didn't care except that we felt bad for our neighbors. Some of them were nice people; stupid, but nice.

Through polycarbonate viewing ports we looked outside the next day. Several zombies could be seen walking the area, aimless in their travels from what we could see. None of them were coming toward our house. None of them had even wandered onto our property. Score one for Travis and his belief that zombies hunted, at least partially, by smell.

Knowing we were secure in our house and prepared to stay for at least a two-week time frame, but not wanting to be stuck inside that long unless we absolutely had to be, AND feeling like we should at least do our part to reduce the zombie outbreak if we could, my wife and I went up into our attic and opened up the gunports we'd installed.

Using my lever action .30-.30 rifle, I engaged every zombie that was within shooting distance. For me that meant about 150 yards if I was going to score reliable head shots. Every head shot I scored literally blew the zombie's head apart, leaving a V-shaped crater at the top of the neck. The first 21 rounds I fired resulted in 19 "dead" zombies. I knew the bodies would need to be destroyed, but I also knew that small scavengers would do some of the work for us.

After a break, my wife and I went up again and stayed for about two hours. In our second attempt, we took out 11 more zombies. After that, both of us went into the bathroom to throw up. Four of the eleven had looked between the ages of ten and fourteen. Just big enough to be infected, but just young and small enough to make us feel like crap for having to do it. We didn't hesitate… but we didn't feel so good afterward.

It was four days before the county health department declared the zombie outbreak quelled. They publicly thanked anyone who had helped but then, in somewhat silly fashion, reminded everyone that carrying guns without a permit was illegal. It didn't make any sense, but that's government for you… of any size I suppose.

FORTIFYING YOUR
HOUSE OR SHELTER

As Justin and his family learned from Travis, fortifying your house against zombies isn't just about making the doors and windows harder to get into. As with any battle strategy, the first goal is to make your house "invisible" to the zombies in the first place. Since their eyesight is poor but they seem to hunt well by scent, the obvious answer is to cover or eradicate your scent as much as possible.

What many people don't realize is that your scent can escape any gap in the seal of your house. Additionally, most folks don't realize just how many "air holes" your house is designed to have.

Using the example of a house built on a crawl space, there's anywhere from one to three feet (or more) of space under the house. That (usually) concrete foundation has several vents in it that are screened and then bracketed over to keep pests out (think small animals like mice, rats, squirrels, raccoons, etc.).

However, nothing about that vent or screen stops the human scent of your house from getting outside the foundation.

In addition to those vent holes that are molded into the concrete foundation, there is usually also a door (or two or more) that allows access to the crawl space. That access door must be fortified and sealed around as well.

The appropriate actions to seal a crawl space include using caulk and duct tape to attach and seal heavy duty plastic sheeting over the inside of the vent holes. The hole should be covered to an excess of two inches in every direction. In general, the holes are too small for a zombie to get through; however, an adolescent sized zombie might get through, so it's necessary to put at least one steel bar across each vent hole either vertically or horizontally and lock it into place with concrete bolts.

The crawl space access door isn't as easy. Prior to sealing it and blocking it shut, you must create an access from inside your home into the crawl space. It's recommended that you create such an access in a closet located centrally in the house. Cut a twenty-inch square hole in the floor between the floor joists and hinge the cut piece. Put TWO sliding bolt locks opposite the hinged side and mount a handle on that same side.

With such access to your crawl space created, you can now seal the outer crawl space access. Begin by using screws at least three inches long to secure the crawl space door frame to the wooden framework it is set in. Once that's done, seal around the crawl space door (inside the crawl space) using caulk, heavy duty plastic sheeting and duct tape just as you did with the vent holes. Once that's done, bolt on steel bars either horizontally or vertically spaced no more than six inches apart and bolted into the concrete foundation on each side of the crawl space access.

For a house built on a basement foundation, the problem is usually basement windows. While they can be pretty well sealed to keep the scent in, they have to be up-armored or otherwise blocked to keep the zombies from breaking them out and (literally) falling into the house head first.

> **NOTE:** While most people don't realize it, zombies tend to hunt in packs. The ones in the back want to get to the prey just as bad as the ones in the front. Just because the ones in the front have gotten to the prey doesn't mean the zombies in the back are stopping. In such instances of a compressed space for a point of entry, every zombie in the back of the pack will keep pressing forward, often times pressing the zombies in the front through whatever opening exists, much like Jello being pushed through a sieve.

Basement windows can be sealed just as the crawl space vent holes were and then steel bars bolted into place either vertically or horizontally spaced no more than six inches apart.

Other vent holes in your house include but are not limited to:

- Your dryer's exhaust vent
- Your over-oven exhaust vent
- Sewage vent pipes for each bathroom
- Drainage vent pipe for your laundry room
- Exhaust fans for each bathroom
- Furnace exhaust (if gas or oil furnace)

Typically, if your house is two stories tall (or taller) these vents are not an issue except those on the ground floor or emanating from the basement (dryer exhaust is the most common basement venting). Any vent that releases gasses from the house less than twenty feet off the ground must be redirected and/or the vent pipe extended so that is vents at least twenty feet or more above the ground.

Studies of air movement in neighborhoods have shown that gasses exhausted from a home twenty feet or more above ground level tend to be drawn UP by drafts of heat that are created by the flocks of homes. Gasses vented out of a house below twenty feet more often than not SINK to ground level and then travel the prevailing wind currents at that level.

Since zombies are rarely seen climbing any structure and, at least as far as has been observed, are not capable of jumping at all, if you can vent all of your scented gasses out of your house above the twenty foot mark, you all but erase your scent from any zombies in the area – at least any scent carried in the air.

Other scents are left when we move about. Just like a dog can track the human scent on the ground or on objects, so can zombies. It is important that any tracks you make to or from your house are erased. This is most easily done by "erasing" them with bleach or ammonia. Both of those smells are strong enough to cover human scent from zombie recognition. Citric acid has also been suggested but not tested in sufficient locations and circumstances to be considered reliable as of this writing.

With every possible scent escape covered or protected, you need to consider actual fortification of your doors and windows. While many people believe that simply dead-bolting your door is sufficient, they form that outlook based on a series of misinformation.

First, the average deadbolt has a "throw" – that's how far the tongue of the bolt actually goes into your door frame – of about one inch. Measure yours. It needs to be a <u>minimum</u> of one inch. More is better.

Second, if the lock plate itself is attached to the door frame with screws less than two inches long, then you're only getting the security of the strength of the facing on the frame. In other words, you're not getting any lock security at all. The lock-plate needs to be attached into the house framing around the door. This usually requires screws of at least a two-inch length; three inches is better.

Third, it's common for entry doors to open IN to your house. That puts the hinges on the inside and keeps anyone from removing the door by taking out the hinge pins. That also means that enough weight or force against the outside of the door can force the door open and IN. Spend the extra dollars to get inset hinges and have the door reversed so it opens OUT. Then, in addition to the long-throw deadbolt and two- or three-inch screws on the lock-plate side, add two slide bolts on the inside of your door: one about six inches from the top and one about six inches from the bottom.

There is a strength to this *and a danger to this*. The strength is that if someone tries to pry your door open from the outside, you have three bolts, each about 2.5 feet apart, holding the door closed against the framework of your house. The danger is that you have three bolts to disengage in a hurry if your house is on fire or if you have another emergency condition inside that you have to escape.

I know it may be common sense, but screen doors, storm doors, sliding glass doors, etc. – *are a waste*. They do not serve to secure your house in any way. That said, a properly fitted storm door does add another layer of insulation from penetrating air.

Now, about your windows. Contemporary architecture includes numerous types of windows on residential homes. Most windows in homes constructed since 1990, or thereabouts, have multiple pains sandwiching an inert gas "bubble" in between them. The windows slide – either up and down or sideways – and have a latch mechanism that is pretty secure; however, unless your windows are made of armored polycarbonate, enough force will break them. Such force can come from natural sources like tree limbs falling or being blown around in a tornado, or that force can come from the pressure caused by several dozen zombies trying to force the one in front through your window. Several tons of zombie flesh is still several tons of force.

At a bare minimum you need to put steel bars across every ground level window of your home. The bars should be at least one inch in diameter and be anchored to your home's frame. If you're mounting them inside that means using the appropriate hardware and screws that are at least three inches long to mount said hardware into the framework of your walls.

The bars should be spaced no more than six inches apart. Remember, zombie goo can still be pushed through broken windows and through those bars which means infected zombie flesh can penetrate your perimeter.

The preferred method of securing windows is to mount metal shutters of steel at least one-quarter inch thick or aluminum at least one-half inch thick so that they can be closed over the window. The shutters are mounted on the outside to either side of the window. You must use four three-inch screws per hinge, and three hinges per shutter half is recommended. When closed, the shutters should cover the entire window plus at least one inch on all sides. To assist with sealing the window, it's recommended that you put a self-adhesive foam strip around the perimeter of the window's exterior so that when the shutters are closed they compress the foam forming a seal around the outer perimeter of the window. When you close the shutters, the slide bolts to secure them will be on the inside. To secure the shutters in a closed and locked position you have to open the window, pull the shutters closed, and slide the bolts into the locked position. For added security, bolts that allow the use of a locking pin or padlock are available.

Windows that are above ground level ("above ground level" defined as at least ten feet from the ground), don't have to be hardened but they still have to be sealed to keep out contamination. Check the fit of all windows to insure that when they are closed you can detect no draft of air around them on either side, the top or the bottom. For the upper floor windows, use clear heavy duty plastic sheeting and duct tape. Cut the sheeting to fit the window plus one inch on all sides. Use the duct tape to hold the plastic sheeting over the interior of the window. When you put the duct tape on, you must pay attention to insure that it overlaps at the corners. After you've put the plastic sheeting in place with a single row of duct tape on each side, add an additional row of duct tape around the outer perimeter of the first row. This redundancy insures a secure hold for the plastic sheeting and reduces to almost nil the chance that you missed a gap around the window that air might get through.

If there is a window in your home that is decorative – that is to say that it doesn't open but merely allows light pass through – it still must be sealed in the event of a zombie outbreak. The concern is not whether or not the glass is airtight but whether the window frame itself is. Use the method described immediately above to seal any decorative windows. If the decorative window is less than ten feet off the ground, it too must be either shuttered or otherwise fortified. Given how small most decorative windows are, it's far easier just to cut a piece of three-quarter inch pressure treated plywood to the appropriate size (the window plus one inch on all sides) and screw it into place. It's recommended that you screw it on the outside. There is no historic record of any zombie manipulating a tool, and if you screw the board up on the inside there is still the chance that outside pressure can push zombie goo through the window with sufficient force to push off the board.

With your house thus sealed and hardened you still have one more concern and it's a doozy: your air-handling unit or units. Yeah. That big metal box with a fan inside that is not supposed to move air in and out of your house but is connected directly to your furnace. In most cases, the "air-handling unit" is both a heat pump and an air-conditioning unit. The quickest and easiest way to reduce your threat of infection via the air-handling unit is to turn it off at the breaker box. That way no accidents happen. The best way is to not only turn off the breaker but also to cover the unit itself with a heavy duty construction trash bag (the 55-gallon size ones often fit) and use duct tape to secure it around the base.

While your house is thus hardened and sealed you must remember two things:

First, there is a limited amount of oxygen in your home. For houses that are two stories or more tall you need to work out a plan to safely and securely perform air exchange via the upstairs windows. Prior to opening the house, you must verify that no zombie contamination exists in your immediate area. Remember that we're talking about sometimes microscopic sized particles.

Second, with no heat or air conditioning running, your house temperature is entirely dependent on the season and the sunlight. Be prepared for temperature extremes accordingly.

8

WE NEVER THOUGHT WE
HAD TO BE THIS CAREFUL

As dictated by Justin Rustovic and notated by Frank Borelli.

One afternoon during a relatively mild local outbreak in our area, we settled in, locked our doors, secured our shutters in place and sat down for an early dinner. One thing that we'd learned: zombies like to be more active at night. No one has ever really figured out why, although, like everything else about them, there must be a scientific reason; something that can be explained.

After dinner we cleaned up the dishes and threw away the leftovers. I realized that the kitchen trash can was full and I needed to take the bag out to our garbage cans. Now, understand: going outside during a zombie outbreak isn't necessarily a bad thing. Yes, if you can avoid it, you should, but if you have to then you have to and, given how slow zombies usually move, it's not a big deal if they're far enough away.

That evening we took all the normal precautions. From our attic viewing ports we checked the area before unlocking the back door. I was ready to go with air mask in place, protective glasses on, fully dressed in jeans and boots with a long-sleeve shirt and gloves. I hadn't taped the wrists because, quite frankly, I was going less than thirty feet to our garbage cans and back. I had my usual Government Model 1911 .45ACP handgun (made by Springfield Armory) in its holster on my belt with two extra magazines. If you counted each bullet as a headshot I had 22 dead zombies on my belt. (Consider the state of existence when these are the protective measures and preparatory steps you have to put in place simply to take out your trash.)

When I got the "all clear" from family members, I quickly unlocked the door, went out with the trash, closed the door securely behind me, heard it being locked, went directly to the trash cans, put the bag in, put the trash can lid back on the can, turned and went back to the house. Everything was timed so I didn't even have to wait to get in.

> **NOTE:** every time a family member or other occupant of a house goes outside during a zombie outbreak you *must* have the outlook that they can be sacrificed if need be to save the rest of the house. That's why the door was locked behind me, and I was surprised not to wait to get in. Normally a visual check has to be done before unlocking the door a second time, but in this case they simply watched me back and forth while scanning the area.

Once I was back in the house the door was relocked, all doors and windows were double checked and we settled for the evening. About a half hour later we heard some noises near our back door and I went to the attic to look out and see what was going on. What I saw gave me chills.

There were four zombies around our trash cans and another one on the steps to our back deck. Steps slow zombies down, but they usually manage to get up them by luck or accident. Personally I believe it's some kind of instinct: if they try to walk and their foot runs into an object they just step higher. It takes them several tries but eventually they'll get their foot up on something. It's almost humorous to watch if the something is higher than, say, a curb or step, but the reality is scary: they CAN come up stairs after you. It just takes them awhile at each step as they make their repetitious attempts, giving you plenty of time to deliver the necessary head shot to put them back down the steps.

I called a warning down to my family about what I was seeing, and my wife went to triple check our back door and windows in that area. I briefly wondered about our crawlspace access door which was right next to our back deck but was 99% sure it was closed, secured and barred. One thing I knew for sure: if it wasn't, there was little I could do about it now.

It's important that you understand our outlook here. Sure, we could have opened the back door and taken the zombies out, or I could have done so from the gun ports in the attic; however, we really didn't want five zombie corpses lying on our back steps or around our trash cans. That's far too much rotting zombie flesh potentially spreading infection within a few feet of the house. Our preference was for them to reach the point of giving up and moving on. That happened about half the time so we had a decent chance we wouldn't have to take them out and we could spare ourselves the close infection chance.

As I thought about our potential course of action, I continued to watch the zombies. Soon another one joined the one at the steps to my deck, and then another… and then another. Before long they had all moved from the trash can to the steps to my back deck. I couldn't figure out what was drawing them from the trash to my back door. I had taken the proper precautions in sealing the house so no smells escaped. I had even treated around the house perimeter with bleach, although I didn't do it daily and it had been a few days.

Finally I saw a sixth zombie coming into the area and walking in their slow stilted way toward my trash cans. He got to them, wandered into them and around them. Then I saw the darnedest thing: he raised his head as if sniffing the air, turned toward my house and walked over to join the rest of the zombies at the bottom of the steps to my deck. Now I had six there but I knew why: a scent trail.

I decided what to do and informed my wife of the plan of action. From the attic, through the closest gunport, I used my Winchester lever-action .30-.30 rifle to shoot each zombie in the head. One shot each was all that was required, and the shots don't alert zombies to the danger of the end of their existence. That said, the high-power rounds do tend to spray zombie head and brain matter all over everything within ten to fifteen feet.

With the six zombies, now mostly headless, sprawled around and on the steps to my deck, I kept watch while my wife and oldest son dressed to go outside. This time they were careful to tape their wrists so there was no gap between gloves and shirt sleeves. Additionally, under their work gloves they wore latex gloves. Instead of regular air masks they wore full protective masks with the attached skirts in place so their necks were covered as well. When they went out, not a single exposed patch of skin existed on either of them.

First, they worked together to spray a fresh layer of bleach around the house. They did the first ring right around the edge of the house, spraying in a pattern that created a swath about three feet wide up against the house. Next they moved out about ten feet from that and sprayed another three-foot swath all the way around. Then they did that again another ten feet out.

After the area had been sprayed down sufficient to (hopefully) cover our scent, they went to work on the zombie corpses. Dragging the zombies at all left bits of zombie flesh on the ground where they were dragged. As much as we hated to move them and create this additional potential contamination, we couldn't burn the bodies right up against the house. We might burn down the house as a result.

The bodies were dragged out to the middle of the concrete pad we had put in some years before as a small basketball court for our son. They were piled together, covered in a fine mist of shaved magnesium under each body, doused in gasoline and then lit. (The magnesium was necessary to make the bodies burn hot enough to destroy the zombie virus; however, you must be careful to not put the magnesium *on top* of the pile of bodies. If you do, two ugly things happen: 1) the magnesium flares up and can blind or burn you, and 2) it doesn't create the necessary temperatures down inside the pile so the zombie virus survives in the ash. The magnesium shavings should be put on top of the first layer of bodies, and then in between each following layer with gasoline going on top of the final layer and all around the bodies.)

Once the bodies were burning, my wife got out our power washer and proceeded to spray down the walls and walkways, steps and deck where the zombies had been shot. The object was to get all of the brain, flesh, hair and other zombie matter off of anything it may have splattered onto. As a safety precaution, she sprayed the area she expected matter may have landed plus about five feet all around it. After power-washing everything, she sprayed it all with ammonia. That served not only to help kill any remaining odor but also rinse the power-washing solution, which contained bleach, off the surfaces where it may actually fade out the color. Yes, even in the midst of a zombie outbreak, people worry about appearances and aesthetics.

As the bodies continued to burn, my wife and son returned to the house, coming in through our laundry room door. We used the laundry room as a contamination clearing area of sorts. In the laundry room they shed their work gloves and put them directly into a burn bag. The gloves had directly touched zombie flesh and therefore carried the virus-infected cells that we couldn't risk having in our home any more than the minimum necessary. Keeping their latex gloves on, and working with some difficulty, they removed their long-sleeved shirts OVER the protective masks and threw them in the burn bag as well.

The "burn bag" as we call it is a construction thickness trash bag that sits inside a steel trashcan with a lock-on lid. We treat it as a bio-hazard containment system. One of our standard operating procedures is that no one opens that trash can unless they have on a protective mask and latex gloves. When clothing items are put into it, they aren't *thrown* in but are set as carefully as possible in so the air inside it is moved as little as possible to minimize the risk of microscopic particles being blown out of the can. Once the lid is sealed back in place, we wait a full five seconds before moving around to let anything that did get blown out settle. When the burn bag is full, we get fully dressed in what we consider "full coverage" clothing and one of us seals the bag, removes the bag, and takes it out to the concrete pad for burning. The first items that go into the next burn bag are the clothing items worn to move the one we just burned.

They took off their boots and set them in the laundry room utility sink which had about an inch of bleach and water in it, mixed one to one. It tended to make the boot soles white but (we hoped) it killed any bits of diseased/infected flesh that might have been picked up by them.

They had no reason to think anything else they had on was infected, so the remainder of their clothing went directly into the commercial grade washing machine we have. They took off the protective masks after taking off their boots, and then my son stripped down while my wife looked away.

NOTE: Zombie outbreaks, like all other pandemic type situations, cause a necessary loss of privacy as people adjust to restricted space living conditions. We did the best we could to preserve each other's privacy given the circumstances.

Once my son had stripped and all his "safe" clothes went into the washer, he grabbed a towel to wrap around his waist and headed for the bathroom to take a shower. My wife stripped down after he'd left that room, put her clothes in the wash and started it using hot water and a hot rinse with double the recommended amount of detergent. Then she too grabbed a towel, wrapped herself and headed for a shower.

As I thought about the events, I realized a couple things. First, we had previously only ever sprayed bleach around the immediate perimeter of the house; we hadn't included the area where our trash cans were, our vehicles were, etc. Second, we had never considered the trail of scent we left going to and from that "safe circle" inside the bleach border. Third, we came to realize that whatever smell was created by the burning of the zombie bodies, it kept other zombies away. We noticed that, during any outbreak, for several days after we burned zombie bodies, no other zombies came within a hundred yards or so of our property.

From that point forward we added some extra precautions to our normal "come and go" routine. As has been noted, we expanded our bleach ring to include the entire perimeter of our property. The outermost ring was in addition to the ring immediately around the perimeter of our house. Also, whenever one of us went out to the trash cans, the wood pile, the vehicles, etc., we took the sprayer with us and we over-sprayed our tracks on the way back. In this fashion we hoped to remove the scent created as our feet moved over the ground. (Hey, if dogs can smell human scent on the ground, how do we know zombies can't?)

We also stopped looking at the burning of zombie corpses as distasteful or a "bad" thing. When zombies were shot, or otherwise stopped, in our neighborhood, we regularly became part of the destruction team. Many a zombie body got burned on our concrete basketball pad. None of our neighbors seemed to realize the effect this had on the other zombies, but we certainly appreciated the added safety space it provided to our house.

By burning those bodies, our bleach rings and other precautions became redundant. Burning those zombie bodies kept the other zombies away. Through trial, error and observation, we noticed that a "zombie burn," as we came to call it, kept other zombies away for about three days. The more bodies we burned, the longer the protection seemed to last with a week being about the maximum effective time. If we only burned one body, the protection seemed to last about 24 hours.

On the one hand, it made good sense to burn as large a pile as possible. On the other hand, burning more than five or six didn't seem to extend the protection time, so there was no need to risk the built up infection pile any longer than necessary. Typically we ended up burning three or four zombies at a time, and sometimes, while the pile was burning, we'd have more bodies to add on.

Once our neighbors began to interact with us about anything zombie related, they also began to realize that we knew a lot more than they did, we were a lot more prepared than they were, and they learned to do what we told them. It was a lesson they all learned the hard way though.

We have one neighbor whose name I won't use. He's somewhat of a hard case: convicted felon, self-employed thug... you know the type. As we took our precautions and other neighbors listened to us, he laughed and told everyone how he'd handle anything the zombies could throw at him. He saw no need to cover his tracks. He refused to spray bleach. He left several zombies to lay where they were in his yard.

He also had two small dogs that he let roam freely. While they were too small to become infected, any mammal can carry the virus. One day we heard shots from inside his house. The story came out that the dogs had gone out and nibbled on a zombie corpse. Then they'd come in and licked his daughter. She happened to have a hangnail and that was all it took for the infection to get into her, kill her and reanimate her, and she started attacking the family.

She bit both her mother and her sister before he realized what he had to do. He had a pump-action shotgun, which he possessed illegally since he was a convicted felon, and he used it. First he blew the head off his zombie-daughter. Then, apparently with very little hesitation according to his surviving son, he also shot and killed his wife and other daughter. As harsh as that seems, it was a smart thing to do. They'd been infected. They *were* going to change. They *would* become zombies. It was safest (not to mention humane) to get them killed and the bodies destroyed.

It was the first time we'd ever had to put infected-but-not-yet-turned dead human bodies onto the zombie fire pile.

After that, he began to pay attention. No more leaving zombie bodies laying around to rot on his property. No more letting the dogs out without having them on a leash. He built a six-foot tall steel mesh fenced in area for them to go outside in.

It wasn't until then that we all realized the value of a chain-link fence. It was a group "DUH" moment. How stupid were we? The next day we were all buying fencing material to put around our properties. Pretty soon we were burning zombie bodies in the streets where they fell after having their heads blown off, smashed in, or run over.

Before the fences had been put up though, we all learned some important lessons.

9

BECOMING "INVISIBLE"

We humans don't often think about it, but we give off an awful lot of "waste." What our body sheds may not actually be what we normally think of as waste, but that's where we need to adjust our thinking. Anything and everything that comes off your body is a waste product that, for all we know, zombies have a way to track or detect. Therefore, in the interest of our own safety and survival, we have to find ways to hide or mask that which we shed.

One of the things many a family dog has done that is annoying is running up to you and jamming their nose in your crotch. We've also watched as they sniff each others' butts. Have you ever wondered why they do these two particular things?

They identify us as much by scent as sight; maybe even more so. Nowhere on our body is there a stronger scent than that which emanates from our genitals. For men, both urine and seminal fluids have distinct and identifiable odors that animals with sensitive olfactory senses can identify individually. Females can be uniquely identified by the smell of their urine and other fluids as well as the change in their scent due to their monthly cycle.

While we may consider it distasteful to even consider such odors, zombies have been shown to have an increased olfactory sensitivity and, therefore, can track us by way of our odors. We must be aware of this and act accordingly. What's that mean?

It means that during a zombie outbreak, perhaps more than any other time, your cleanliness is vital. That said, we must also be aware of the aroma of any product we use in the cleansing process.

Clean water is a neutral scent to all mammals. To zombies it doesn't matter at all. Water has no effect on or meaning to zombies, so the scent doesn't matter to them. That said, we need to recognize that the soap we use, the deodorant we put on, the shampoo, conditioner, cologne, lotion, oil, etc., all have their own unique scents – and no other mammal out there uses them. Anything manmade we use to alter our body's scent signature actually adds to that signature and makes us *more*, not less, detectable to zombies.

Now, while it's impossible to completely mask our scent (ask any hunter who has tried it), we can minimize the artificial scent we give off as well as our own body odor. To minimize our body odor, we simply need to stay clean. Bathe in fresh running water using a basic unscented soap that contains no deodorant. If you sniff your soap, you should smell no odor or aroma at all. If *you* do, a zombie certainly will.

Wash your clothes using a non-scented detergent and run all clothing through two rinse cycles. Do not use fabric softeners in the wash or the dryer.

Do not use cologne, body lotion, deodorant, etc. It's better to have to take two showers each day than to walk around advertising through your scent, "Here I am!! Come kill me!"

Aside from the scent your body gives off, there has been some theoretical discussion as to whether or not zombies can detect the higher heat signature of a living human as compared to the reduced heat signature of other zombies or smaller mammals.

This question has never really been settled and remains an open issue. Some "experts" believe that there's no way zombies could tell the difference between one of their own or a living human simply by the difference in heat signature. Further, they don't believe a zombie could tell the difference between a human and a dog by the heat signature each has.

Others believe that if it might even be a remote possibility then we should take protective action against it. Obviously we can't change our heat signature, and even the military has had only minor success at hiding a body's heat profile. There are some synthetic treatments that can be applied to clothing that help contain or hide the heat signature of the person wearing said clothing; however, the treatment requires ongoing special handling of the clothing and isn't cheap. Since so much clothing gets contaminated and has to be destroyed, the cost of treatment has been deemed prohibitive.

One thing most do agree on is that zombies can find larger clusters of people. For instance, recorded attacks on apartment buildings are much higher than attacks on single-family homes. The recorded number of attacks on shopping malls is higher than the number of attacks on libraries. Zombies obviously go for the larger groups of potential food targets: humans in their most densely populated social areas.

What we can do is hide the heat signature of these structures better than we do. Earlier in this book we discussed how to seal a home's windows and doors. Those same protective measures can be taken to minimize ambient heat flow in and around the buildings where we socialize. Doing so will minimize or at least decrease the number of attacks that occur on such protected structures.

Something else we don't often think about is the scent our waste products give off. We mentioned urine earlier, but what about those butt-sniffing dogs? All of us are aware that feces stink. Why don't we think about the scent given off by our septic systems? Our sewage systems? Our waste treatment facilities and more?

If you have a septic system on your property, it has two openings: the main opening near the middle of the tank, and an access for cleaning at one end. The access is always above ground while the main opening may be as much as two feet below ground level. *Any septic opening or access that is above ground can be smelled by zombies and is a clear indicator of human presence.*

The easy answer is to cover that access to keep the smell from getting out. The danger of that is that methane and other flammable gases are released from your septic tank and if you completely seal it, those gases can build up in a dangerous way. What's the answer?

Remember earlier in the book when we talked about venting smells from inside your house at least twenty feet above ground? We need to do the same thing with the septic access points. A typical septic access is about ten inches in diameter. Get a sufficient length (or lengths) of PVC pipe that is twelve inches in diameter. Place it vertically around your septic access and vent those gases up at least to the roofline height of your house. If your main septic access is exposed to the air, construct a pyramid-shaped box to put over it with a ten- or twelve-inch circular opening at the top. Place your PVC pipe on top of that and brace it as necessary. Again, make sure your pipe extends up at least as high as your roofline.

In and around your home, when you come and go, you leave a trail. Not only do you shed dead skin cells that zombies (and dogs and other animals) can smell, but you also change the smell of the ground you walk on so that it's different from the ground around it. This is especially true on any ground that has organic growth such as grass or plants. Therefore, everywhere you walk, you leave a trail.

If you're traveling through an area, that's not such a big deal. Yes, a zombie could follow you, but if you continue to move, it's unlikely he'll catch you; however, if you leave a trail to and from your home constantly, there's the chance that your smell is leading zombies straight to your door.

The way to avoid this is to regularly douse any area you travel with bleach or ammonia. As has been described, a typical liquid sprayer makes this easy and efficient. The goal is to leave no discernable trail to follow.

It's been theorized that one day zombies might learn that the smell of bleach or ammonia means a human has been in the area, but it's not commonly believed that will ever happen. First, the zombies would have to be able to pass information from one to another, and they've displayed no communication skills beyond modeled behavior. Second, they'd have to live long enough to learn about the smell of bleach or ammonia during multiple hunts or encounters. Most zombies, once detected, don't "live" that long; they tend to get destroyed pretty quickly to minimize their threat and the exposure of humans in the area to the virus. Third, it's never been proven that zombies are capable of learning anything at all. Usually their bodies consume themselves, the muscles atrophying constantly, before zombies have enough time to commit more than a few hunts, provided the humans are aware and prepared.

Finally, it's been observed that, for whatever reason, zombies tend to avoid areas where large firefights have occurred. Where there's a large amount of spent brass on the ground, the zombies tend to walk around a given area; however, the exact opposite is also true.

For some reason, where only one or two shots have been fired, zombies seem to use those shooting spots as beacons to follow, like bread crumbs on a trail. So, if you encounter a zombie and shoot it with any kind of weapon that ejects spent brass casings, it's imperative that you pick up the brass if you can. That spent brass, if you leave it, will provide a trail for other zombies to follow, and it will always lead in your general direction.

10

WHO KNEW ZOMBIES
COULD HUNT?

As dictated by Justin Rustovic and notated by Frank Borelli.

If you've ever watched any zombie movie at all, you've seen the zombies mindlessly shambling in a random direction, looking rotted away as they go. Then again, in some movies the faces aren't so rotted and you can clearly see the eyes; the attention and awareness in the actors' faces. But that's just movies. From them we "learn" (as if fiction is an accurate portrayal of reality) that if we can just run fast enough far enough, we'll always get away.

So, here's a question for you: if the zombies are simply wandering mindlessly and we can always outrun them, why do so many people get killed by them? Or, worse yet, converted into them? And where are they wandering mindlessly to?

The answer is, there's a limit to their "wandering mindlessly." Once they find human scent or spore, the wandering stops and the pursuit begins. We learned this at first through the mistakes we saw others make. Then, having come to a working hypothesis – that zombies did indeed hunt – we researched and studied their behavior very carefully. We were proven correct.

The good news is that we can easily outrun them if we use our heads. The bad news is that they aren't stopped until they are destroyed, and we have to be careful about how we do that. Too many movies "taught" us that it was okay to shoot them at close range, or bludgeon them with a bat at arms' reach, and get covered with zombie gore in the process. The movies were wrong – as has been discussed in previous chapters. Zombie hunting is a practiced and careful art. The challenge is being an artist while running for your life or trying to protect the lives of your family members.

Like any other predator, zombies like to hunt in a target-rich environment. That's why cities are so quickly overrun. The dense population of cities offers zombies a greater chance of "catching" their prey, not to mention the attraction of the scent and spore of hundreds of thousands, if not millions, of live humans with warm fresh blood pumping through their veins and brains just fired up with electrochemical impulses.

Our first hint that zombies could hunt came when one of our neighbors got a visit from some out-of-state family. I had to tip my hat to the travelers simply because they had taken the risk of travelling through an infested area for the sake of visiting family.

NOTE: Many readers will be surprised to find out that the government permitted free movement during a zombie outbreak rather than closing down surface roads and highways to limit the potential spread of the infection. What the government at all levels finally learned was that road blocks attract zombies and there are far too many back roads and optional routes for the limited manpower available to be able to stop people from getting where they were determined to go.

So anyway, the neighbor's family showed up and about an hour later came a group of zombies walking along the same path of travel. It didn't dawn on us at first that the zombies might have been tracking the carload of human bodies because zombies have always, in our experience, tended to walk the path of least resistance… roadways. But then we thought about it: to get onto our road the zombies had to make several turns, and then when they got onto our street, we watched them make the turn to go toward our neighbor's house using exactly the same path the car had driven and with no humans showing in the area.

The zombie group numbered about ten, so destroying them wasn't a challenge. After alerting our neighbor to what was coming his way, we advised him NOT to shoot the zombies and that we'd be doing that from behind them. What we needed he and his family to do was watch the area around us from their second floor firing positions. He understood and agreed. Then we called the neighbors between our house and his and let them know what was going on. They all said they understood as well.

With everyone on the same page so we didn't get "accidentally" shot in the head, we suited up, armed ourselves and headed out. It was pretty easy to take out the ten zombies with head shots. We were able to approach within about twenty feet of them before we started shooting, and we confirmed our estimated count of ten. It was my wife and I shooting which meant five zombies each except that I recover from each shot slightly faster than she does so I shot six to her four. I was using a lever-action .30-.30 and each shot, at that distance, pretty much disintegrated the zombie head on impact. My wife was shooting a pump-action twelve gauge and was using 4-shot loads. Each zombie head she shot received several dozen lead balls at high velocity. Those heads were pretty much pulped and splattered, quite thankfully away from us.

Once the zombies were all down, the bodies had to be collected and burned. Since my wife and I were already suited up and properly armed, as was agreed during the previous phone calls, we held security positions at either end of the area around where the zombie bodies were lying, and our neighbors came out to "clean up." Cleaning up, at that point, essentially meant stacking the bodies with magnesium shavings between them, dousing them in gasoline and then lighting the stack on fire. While it burned, they sprayed the entire area around it with ammonia.

After everything had been taken care of and we were back secure in our house, we discussed the zombie mob's behavior was we cleaned our guns. Between my wife and I, we decided to pay more attention to the movement of the zombies any time we encountered one while we were out and about.

Various opportunities presented themselves across the span of the next several months. When there were no reported outbreaks in our area, we'd do our best to go out shopping or for an "evening out." Even in the midst of potential zombie pandemics, life goes on and we do what we can to keep things normal. While many businesses had closed down after the first big outbreak, several more started in their place. The people who closed shop often moved to less populated areas and tried to make a go of isolated farming/hunting to survive. Some made it… some didn't. Of those that didn't, I don't know what was worse – those who succumbed to starvation or those who became zombies/zombie victims themselves.

At any rate, while my wife and I were out, we had four occasions to watch zombies in action while we maintained positions of relative safety. In the first two instances it was clear that the zombies were tracking the intended victims. Thankfully the zombies were taken out before they made direct infection-transmitting contact with any humans.

In the third instance, we saw what we were afraid we'd see: there were five zombies total. Two of them were "in pursuit" of humans while the other three approached from a flanking position. We would never have recognized this group hunting behavior if we hadn't 1) been looking for it, and 2) observed the entire incident beginning before the humans realized they were being hunted. It never ceases to amaze me, with all of the informational material out there, how little some people know about how to avoid becoming an attractive target to zombies. For the record, the third instance ended well. The zombies were all destroyed, but since it was in a public parking lot, the country HAZMAT team came out to collect the zombie corpses to transfer them to the local crematorium. The truly important lesson to be learned, in hindsight after the fact, was that two zombies were serving as "chasers" driving the intended human targets toward the flanking zombies that would ambush them. There was simply nothing we'd been taught, or had ever seen in the mainstream media material about zombies, that prepared us for that realization.

In the fourth instance, we actually saw zombies turn and walk *away* from their intended targets in an apparent attempt to improve the ease of their approach. In other words, they demonstrated an awareness of their own mobility challenges and walked away from their targets, taking a longer route back, but one with fewer obstacles which had the net effect of making their approach easier.

With some neighbors over one evening, we discussed all of the information and decided that before we jumped to the conclusion that zombies could hunt we would have to more closely study the behavior for ourselves. That alone is a dangerous undertaking. To do so we'd have to expose ourselves in multiple groups and move around in such a way as to allow the zombies the opportunity to display the behavior without us actually prompting it out of them by accident.

That's how, on one dreary Saturday morning in a southern county in our state where an outbreak had been reported, my wife and I along with seven of our neighbors were suited up, armed and out to accomplish or mission. With nine of us total, we broke up into three pairs and one trio and set out along our predetermined travel path. Our goal was to find at least five zombies that we could bait that would follow one of our pairs.

Then the other pairs/trio could follow and observe the zombies. The one extra operative rule that we put into effect was that any one of us could decide the situation was too hazardous, that the risk of infection was growing too great, and that the zombies involved would receive immediate head shots.

Within an hour, my wife and I had two zombies following us. Our travel path was on a dirt road that gave them no obstacles, but it presented none to us either, and our muscles weren't rotting away. We managed to stay about thirty yards ahead of them – not getting too far ahead and not letting them get close enough that we'd be sprayed with zombie matter either if any of our friends shot one.

Via radio we let our compatriots know what was going on and were comforted to hear everyone else converging in our direction. Before our friends got close, we had another zombie come wandering out of the woods behind us and fall in with the other two. Three zombies on our trail. No big worry… yet.

Then, about a half mile farther down the road, we found ourselves in somewhat of a predicament: two zombies came out of the woods in front of us, moving in our direction. Although there were woods to our right, there was an open field to our left, so we had plenty of room to move with acceptable visibility around us. We got on the radio and let our friends know what was going on. I was relieved to hear that several of them – one pair and the trio – had us in their sights and could see the zombie behavior.

The two zombies that had been in front of us turned to follow us into the field, just as the three zombies behind us did in almost mirror fashion. Five zombies on our trail now. They didn't move as easily across the field due to defects in the terrain and the almost-waist-high grass that was growing there.

We had gone about 150 yards through the field when we were surprised by three zombies standing up almost directly in front of us, less than five yards away. They had been crouching in the grass, waiting for our arrival. That was my limit on acceptable risk. My rifle came up almost instinctively as I barely slowed down my steps. My first shot hit a zombie in his left cheek, blowing his head into a mix of gray flesh, bone and pudding-like brain matter at almost the same time my wife's shotgun delivered even greater devastation to another. The third one's head disappeared into a fine gray mist as my bullet and her shotgun shell load impacted it at the same time.

The engagement took less than two seconds, but we had no idea how much distance had been crossed by the zombies behind us in that time. We stopped, turned and brought our weapons up to start destroying whatever was on our trail. Instead of five zombies we saw eight, and they'd closed the distance to about twenty yards.

I levered through five shots as fast as I could accurately place them. My wife would have joined in the shooting but with four-shot loads in her Remington shotgun, a head-sized target twenty yards away might not get properly destroyed or sufficiently destroyed to stop the zombie. She waited until they'd gotten less than ten yards away before she fired a shot. I'd shot five in that time and had to reload my rifle's tubular magazine. I began loading fresh rounds in as she fired her first round, worked the action on her shotgun and fired the second.

The last zombie was getting a little close for engagement. We didn't want his gore splattered on us; the risk of infection was too high.

We turned and began to jog across the field in front of us, circling slightly around the zombies we'd killed and were startled when another two stood up in the grass less than ten feet away. I remember wondering where the hell my friends were. I also remember thinking that the idea of zombies hunting was no longer a theory or hypothesis. These had set up a multiple layer ambush and hidden in wait.

My wife fired from the hip as we moved, obliterating one zombie's head. I was still reloading when they'd stood up and almost dropped the round in my hand. I managed to bobble it into my palm in the right position, stuff it into the magazine, work the lever and bring my gun up to engage the other zombie in front of us. As I did, I heard my wife's shotgun boom beside me, but she wasn't shooting at the same zombie I was.

Smart lady, she had turned and engaged the last zombie that had been chasing us. In less than a minute's time we'd destroyed – or at least stopped – thirteen zombies. We still had to pile them up in the road and call the HAZMAT team to come destroy the bodies. If we left the corpses lying around the small scavenger mammals would come nibble on them and become carriers of the infection. Such would only serve to potentially spread the already pandemic level infection.

I was still wondering where our friends were when several shots rang out from the woods across the road we'd been walking on before we were chased into the field. Moving back across the field, but this time with a little more caution, we tried to raise our friends on the radio as we went. We got no response and found ourselves trying to follow the sound of shots as we also called the zombie kill in to the local authorities.

At the road, we followed the sound of shots, very hesitantly, into the woods. We moved carefully trying to be alert to any sound… any movement around us. After about one hundred yards or so we became aware of others in the woods, but we didn't know if it was other humans or more zombies. We paused and looked around, doing our best to blend into the trees we were standing next to. I tried the radio again.

One of my neighbors answered finally. They were still a couple hundred yards away from us. They had also been hunted and had been driven into an ambush. They were just finishing up the necessary head shots and would be coming to join us shortly.

We turned and made our way carefully back to the road. We stood in the middle, back to back, each of us responsible for a 180-degree swath of space in front of us. As we waited for our friends, we watched, and shot, several zombies who walked out of the woods into the roadway. Seven was the final total for that group. We continued to stand.

In another few minutes we heard the clop clop clop sound of a horse's hooves on the ground, steadily getting stronger as the horse got closer. Around a small curve in the road came a horse and buggy which is not an unusual sight for the area. Amish folks are still a significant portion of the population in our area, and we are constantly amazed that they haven't all been killed or infected since they don't use guns and are hardly willing to fight, even in defense of their lives.

The horse and buggy kept coming, staying to the right side of the road, or the left half from our perspective. I couldn't see anyone in the buggy, and when I asked my wife, she couldn't either.

As we were watching the horse and buggy get steadily closer I realized that we were distracted from watching the tree line for any zombies that might come wandering out. Additionally, we made the mistake of both looking in the same direction. We had no rear security.

With that realization, I spun around and found four zombies nearly on top of us. All of them were in Amish clothing, and the straggly steadily rotting beards of the men grew only from their chins; no mustaches. One was female – or had been – and was in a tattered light blue dress with a matching bonnet still on her head.

The engagement distance was too close for my liking, but we didn't have a lot of choice. The damn horse and buggy had stopped close to us and had veered into the middle of the small roadway. Moving quickly around it might have been accomplished, but there were too many questions about it in general to do so without caution.

So, engagement it was. My rifle barked. My wife's shotgun boomed. Amish zombie heads disintegrated in front of us. Although I didn't see any back splatter come toward us and I didn't feel any such impact me, I was silently thankful for my protective mask and neck covering as well as my long sleeves, double layer of gloves and taped down wrist closures.

That seemed to be it for the zombies at that time. When we started shooting, the horse turned away from us and trotted off with the apparently empty buggy bouncing along behind it. Our friends finally came out of the woods, and we got the necessary calls in to the local authorities (again) as well as the state HAZMAT team. We also alerted the local animal control folks to the possibility of the stray horse wandering around dragging an empty buggy behind it.

We all headed home, decontaminated and then gathered for a meeting about what had happened. The consensus was that zombies were most definitely capable of hunting and not just simple hunting either. They were capable of planning, strategy and team work.

We wrote up a report on the day's activities and I faxed it to the local sheriff's office. We didn't really expect the authorities to take us seriously because they seemed to readily dismiss anyone or anything that disagreed with their official position on anything. We also felt morally obligated to submit it. If they ignored it, that was their problem.

FOOD & WATER STORAGE & PROTECTION

Much of the required security for protecting water supplies cannot be accomplished by the average person. It requires action on the part of the water supply companies. That said, if you have your own well, then there are some precautions you should take to avoid infection.

There are (essentially) two types of wells people tend to have on their property: Open and sealed. Open wells are what we think of when we see the covered, wood frame surrounded well with a bucket on a rope that has a hand crank to raise and lower it. Sealed wells have either a hand pump or an electric pump. Sealed wells are not immediately open to contamination, especially if they're drawn from aquifers. Open wells are (obviously) open to contamination. *For the sake of your personal safety, it is wise to purify water from either one prior to use for cleaning or consumption.*

The process for purifying water for use applies to water from sealed wells, open wells, cisterns, rain barrels, etc. First, assume that any water you have not previously purified isn't and that you need to purify it prior to any use.

Second, recognize that contaminated water is as dangerous to use for bathing or cleaning as it is to consume. You should not even use water you haven't purified to wash your pets, and you certainly shouldn't let your pets drink it. Any place on your body that is a mucus membrane or has an open wound, no matter how small, is an access point for the zombie virus.

Third, realize that when clean purified water is scarce, there are people who will happily kill you to get it from you. We can all live for several days without food, but 72 hours without water will kill most of us. The other side of that fact is that 24 hours after drinking contaminated water you'll be "dead" and beginning the change into a zombie.

Finally, understand that because of that premium value placed on clean purified water, realize that "water security" isn't just making sure your water is clean before using it but also means protecting whatever purified water supply you have. The value of water applies whether it's been purified or not; however, purified water is of greater value and is a larger target. Unfortunately, for the desperate, there is no way to know the difference.

You see, people are a sneaky and conniving bunch. I've known people who treat their purified water as more valuable than guns and bullets and secure it accordingly. To some extent they are correct in their outlook. Of course,

I've also known people who stored ALL water in such a fashion, purified or not.

Collecting water isn't hard; after all, Mother Nature offers plenty depending on the climate you live in. We call it "rain." That said, you have to collect it, store it, purify it and then store that. Collection is relatively easy but amounts to having a number of open wells around your house.

To do this you need one construction-weight 55-gallon plastic drum for each downspout you plan to collect from. If, for whatever reason, your house doesn't have downspouts, you can build a water trap lid using any wide-mouth catcher that feeds into a smaller outlet.

Do the math on rain collection and prepare accordingly. If the area you live in gets an annual average rain fall of twelve inches (that's one foot of rain per year) and your roof is three-hundred square feet in area, then you've got approximately 300 cubic feet of water rolling off your roof each year. As a *very* rough way of visualizing this, one gallon of liquid is *about* one cubic foot. It's actually smaller, so that $300ft^3$ is *more* than 300 gallons of water.

As an example, Maryland (selected at random) averages 42 inches of rainfall per year. That's 3.5 feet. Multiply that by the $300ft^2$ of rooftop and you get $1,050ft^3$ of water annually. Historical documents show that Maryland has had a record rainfall year over 60 inches which would have provided close to 2,000 gallons of water from that $300ft^2$ roof top. Maryland has also had a year where only 20 inches of rain fell, which would have produced less than 500 gallons of water. Plan for the worst; be pleasantly surprised by anything better that happens.

On a typical house there is a downspout at each corner, so if you place a collection drum at each downspout you have the capacity to collect 220 gallons of water. Prior to placing the drums, you need to consider how you plan to get water out of them. At any hardware store you can get taps to put into the drums. Those taps have faucet-type outlets with threads set up to screw on garden hoses. Gravity is a wonderful tool if you plan ahead and use it. Saving stress on your back is also a good thing. So, here's what you do.

Using 2x10s and ¾" pressure treated plywood, build a platform for each drum. The platform height should be about 2.5 to 3 feet off the ground. Given that water weighs, on average, about eight pounds per gallon and you plan on collecting 55 gallons (440 pounds of water), build your platform with suitable strength and stability. Insure that your platform is level both in structure and in placement. It may seem trivial, but if the platform is not level, then the collection barrel won't be level and this will cost you capacity at the top. Pray you never find out the hard way, but water is precious and you don't want to waste any or lose any because your barrel isn't level.

Put a tap with an on/off lever or knob into the bottom of the barrel and situate the platform/barrel so the downspout feeds into the barrel. Just so you don't get every leaf, nut, twig, etc., into your water, on top of the barrel put a rough filter.

The filter should be metal or plastic mesh screen covered with about two inches of that white filter material that goes into fish tank water filters. It just helps filter out some of the finer pieces of yuck before the water gets to the screen mesh and then into your barrel. Obviously any open space at the top of the barrel should be covered either by the filter or some material that keeps debris from falling in. Few things suck more than having to disassemble your water barrel to clean out the tap – from the inside.

Remember, *this water is not clean, nor is it purified*. It has washed off your roof along with every scrap of bird poop, squirrel urine, etc. It has been *roughly* filtered and, at a bare minimum, needs to be purified before you use it to cook or wash with. In a zombie-infested environment it would be okay as a water source only for animals small enough not to change; however, they can still be carriers of the virus, and you need to act accordingly.

So after you've collected this roughly filtered water, you need to clean it properly. Many companies make decent water filtration devices sufficient to your need. Higher quality filters remove smaller sized contaminants. Many a person has said, "This one is good enough," as they considered price versus quality. If you find yourself in that quandary there is one thought you should carefully consider: *What's your life worth?*

Invest in a good filtration system and purchase at least a dozen replacement filters for it. Most of them have a filter set up or rated for 1,000 gallons of water. Look at your family/group size and estimate your need. Every emergency preparedness reference in the world says you need at least one gallon per person per day. That's one gallon for consumption, cooking and hygiene. One gallon per person per day. If you have a family of five then you need five gallons per day. If you have pets, add one-half gallon for each of them per day. Multiply your daily need by 365 and figure out how much water per year you might have to filter.

Example: Household with mom, dad, son, daughter, dog and cat. Mom = 1 gallon. Dad = 1 gallon. Son = 1 gallon. Daughter = 1 gallon. Dog = ½ gallon. Cat = ½ gallon. That makes the household a five-gallon-per-day household, and then only in emergency ration circumstances. Five gallons per day equals 1,825 gallons per year. Again, that's only if emergency ration circumstances and controls are in place. The typical family uses a lot more than that. As a general rule of thumb, if you're using the water out of your collection barrels as your primary water supply then emergency rationing should be in place.

It's easy to see, using that example, why you would need multiple filters for your water filtration system. Admittedly you're starting out with fresh water (rain water) so the filters may last longer, but plan on using them only for the rated amount/limits. That means two filters per year minimum for most households.

After the water has been filtered it must then be purified. These are two separate steps in the process, and both must be completed if you plan on using the water to consume, cook with or use for personal hygiene. No one has been yet able to confirm whether or not filtration completely removes the zombie virus from water; however, it has been conclusively proven that water boiled for ten minutes *does* kill any virus particles that may be present.

Therefore, once you have collected, rough filtered and then fine filtered your water, you must boil it for ten minutes.

> **NOTE:** That's ten minutes at a "rolling boil," not a bare boil. Again, it's only your life, so don't be in a hurry or stingy with energy. Boil it – hard for at least ten minutes. If you boil it longer, you only lose volume as the water boils away into steam.

> **NOTE:** Do not attempt to collect the steam by condensing it under a hood, etc. Steam can be formed as soon as the water is hotter than room temperature. It is NOT safe for use, and if you do collect it, you must insure that it's purified before use.

Once your water has been collected, rough filtered, fine filtered and purified by boiling, you must store it in clean containers. Clean containers are those which have been cleaned using anti-bacterial soap and water at a temperature of at least 120°F or higher. Don't scald yourself in the process. Once filled with water, the container must be sealed with an equally clean lid. Once sealed, if the container is opened before it's empty, the water it holds must be purified by boiling again as a safety measure.

As was mentioned earlier, water isn't light. At about eight pounds per gallon, even if you're storing your clean water in five-gallon containers, that's about forty pounds per container. It is recommended that you store these containers up off the ground which means placement on a sufficiently strong and level shelf or other such structure. Until you are going to use the water out of a given container, keep the taps covered, especially if you have any pets in the house. If they get thirsty they may smell the water and lick the taps in an attempt to get some. Even if they are small enough not to become zombiefied themselves, they can still carry the virus. If they lick the taps, any water flowing out of the taps could then become infected.

If this all sounds a bit paranoid, it probably is. But we are, after all, only discussing your life. Finally, keep the amount of purified water you have stored a secret secure inside your family. As was said: water is a precious commodity and people will kill for it. Don't make yourself or your family a target unnecessarily.

12

WHAT WE SAW HAPPEN TO OUR NEIGHBORS

As dictated by Justin Rustovic and notated by Frank Borelli.

In the midst of a hot summer, a couple weeks after a recent zombie outbreak in our area, the local water company shut down operations for day so that they could drain and clean all the delivery pipes before returning to normal operations. Anyone with half a brain (and still human) purified everything that came out of the tap anyway, but getting (assumed) clean water to start with was still easier than collecting your own.

Well, if you were the kind of family that was already keeping a supply of safe water on hand anyway, then one day of no water from the tap was no big deal. Even if you were a family that was aware of the emergency water supplies typically in the average home, then you'd do okay for a day. After all, most homes have a 40-gallon hot water heater (or larger), and at least two toilets with tanks that held three or more gallons each. That alone is 46 gallons of water with zero preparation – if you know about it and think about it. Most homes also have a tub or two and each will hold 40 gallons or more if you take the time to fill them before the water supply is turned off.

It also helps if you pay attention to your local news so that you know about any planned interruptions in the water supply service.

We have… well, had a neighbor family that did just about everything wrong they could where water was concerned. First, they never collected any water at all. They left themselves 100% dependent on the local water service. Second, they didn't pay attention to the news so they were completely ignorant of the planned water cut off. Third, as a result of their ignorance, they kept using water – after the supply had been cut off – just like the water was still in endless supply. Fourth, the water company's "one day cut off" ended up being seven days due to unexpected events that they had no control over. Finally, when that unprepared family ran out of water and began to reach the limits of endurance where their thirst was concerned, they went to local outdoor bodies of water – such as our community's lake.

Admittedly the lake was a fresh water lake, but they didn't filter it and they didn't boil it as far as anyone knows. We don't know who the first person in the house to die and change was either. What we DO know is that about three days after the scheduled water outage occurred they were calling around asking all of us for water. None of us is cruel, but the first rule of survival is that you *only* help others who have initially helped themselves, and you *never* help anyone at a cost to you and your family's survival expectation.

So, while they got a few gallons here and there, most of us turned them away quite apologetically. The man, Chris, made some threats to me when I told him I wouldn't help him. I told him he could take as much as fifty gallons out of any one of my rain barrels but he had to have his own containers to transport it in and he'd have to do all the fine filtering and purification himself. His problem was that he had no filtration equipment and his family was all so thirsty that waiting for the water to boil and cool was difficult at best.

At any rate, they ended up taking five-gallon construction buckets down to the local lake in the bed of his pickup truck. They loaded up each bucket by dipping it in the lake and then putting it in the back of the truck. They drove home – about two miles – around twists and turns and over bumps, etc. and ended up at home with about half the water having spilled out of the buckets. That only added to their frustration.

Then they took those buckets of unfiltered water into their house and began boiling it in one-gallon pots. We'll never know if they didn't boil it enough or if someone got some of the unpurified water in an open wound or if someone simply lost their patience, gave in to their thirst and took a drink of the unpurified water.

What we do know is that about two days after their water gathering jaunt to the lake, about five days after the scheduled water shutdown, they all came out of the house zombies.

Chris and his wife had changed in their sleep if I had to guess. He was wearing just a pair of boxers, and she was in a night shirt that was just long enough to cover her private areas. The kids were hard to look at. The daughter was nine, if I remember correctly. She wandered out, milky white eyes, straggly dead hair, grayish skin, hands with cracked fingernails raised and waving gently as she walked. She was dressed for school from the looks of it: jeans, a long-sleeve pull-over blouse and her school bag of books. The son was in high school and, as much of a shame as it was to look at him, it was also humorous. He had also apparently been dressed for school which involved tennis shoes not tied on his feet, baggy jeans not secured around his waist, a t-shirt that was a size too small and barely reached his waist, and some kind of knit skull cap that he wore even on hot summer days. The humorous part was that his jeans were bunched around his ankles because he was apparently too stupid – even before he became a zombie – to figure out how a belt worked. As a result, he shuffled along with his tennis shoes and jeans dragging. He couldn't lift his feet far because the shoes would fall off and, for whatever reason, he appeared to have an awareness of that. He did not, however, seem to care that his jeans were around his ankles and the whole world could see his boxers which were a bright lime green color with, of all things, zombie faces all over them. (Such clothing had been a big fad prior to actual outbreaks occurring.)

Our house phone rang that morning. It was one of our other neighbors – those who live directly across from Chris' house – letting us know what was going on. We looked out our windows and saw them. Of course, our neighbors all had one question: "What do we do?" None of them could stomach the thought of "killing" neighbors. They called me and asked because they believed I'd do it without hesitation. They were right.

Ten minutes later I was suited up and armed properly with my pump shotgun. Since there were only four of them, I was going out alone. It only makes sense to risk as few lives as possible and, as slow as zombies move, a skilled and disciplined shooter can take out quite a few of them in a relatively short period of time.

At any rate, I was ready to go with my protective mask on, neck shield, long sleeve shirt, double gloves, taped wrists, jeans and boots with the ankles taped as well. I had the shotgun with eight rounds in it and eleven more at hand. I didn't expect to need more than four.

I anticipated shooting the first two from at least twenty yards away so I had loaded the first two rounds of my shotgun with an ammo called PolyShok. It was manufactured by a company that had gone out of business prior to the first publicly recognized outbreaks. After the government finally admitted and acknowledged the risks, PolyShok was revived with a huge investment of government dollars.

What's so special about this ammo you ask? It was a tail-stabilized twelve gauge round which made it pretty accurate. I knew I could easily hit head shots from 25 yards away or more. The projectile was a single plastic cup of shaved lead that delivered about 1,000 foot pounds of energy to the target. It also opened on impact and splashed the shaved lead around like shrapnel coming out of a grenade. The full energy delivery was 100% inside of eight inches, and body tissue within eight inches of the entrance wound was fully pulped.

After those first two rounds, I had double-ought ammo. Each of those rounds held nine .32-caliber lead balls which were launched out of the gun at about 1,100 feet per second. Combined, they did a fair amount of damage and would mostly remove a zombie's head from its body.

Almost the moment I was out of my house I heard the door slam and triple lock behind me. A few sparse moments later the four zombies turned toward me. Did they smell me? Did they hear and react to the sound of the door opening and closing? Who knows? Who cares? I had four zombies coming my way; people I knew and used to enjoy the company of. I approached them with a purpose – much as they approached me, but I did it a lot quicker.

When I got what I estimated to be 25 yards from the Chris zombie, I leveled the shotgun. For some reason, a quote from the owner and designer of the PolyShok round came to mind. "*Life is a food chain. If you're not at the top, you're on the menu.*" With that thought in mind I clicked off the safety, sighted and fired. The PolyShok round made an ugly hole just under the Chris zombie's left eye. The hole was about ¾" in diameter, and I saw the effects of energy delivery in an explosive way. The Chris zombie's eye literally pulped and then blew out of the eye socket, a mass of gray and white material that seemed to come out like an apple that had been hit by a sledge hammer. At almost the same moment, more gray goo sprayed out of both of the zombie's ears. Oddly enough, the cranium stayed intact; however, the brain had been pulped, as had been demonstrated by the collected mess of it that had been forcefully ejected from both ears.

Working the action on my shotgun, I adjusted my aim to point at Chris' wife, Shelby. I fired my second shot and watched as the PolyShok round entered her right eye socket, and brain goo, along with other miscellaneous matter, flew out of both her ears and her left eye socket. Silently I admitted to myself how impressed I was with the energy delivery. Some of her brain goo had flown at least ten feet. In an equally silent fashion, I was thankful that I'd started this engagement so far away.

I pumped the shotgun again and turned my sights on the next closest zombie – the daughter. Although the son was valiantly trying to make it to me, his jeans around his ankles simply didn't allow him to travel at even normal zombie speed which is, in and of itself, slow. I felt a twinge of regret as my sights settled onto the little girl zombie's face. Taking careful aim, I triggered off that round and stood in awe of the difference upon impact of the nine .32-caliber projectiles.

One moment that little girl was standing there, walking in her zombie shuffle manner toward me. The next moment, the zombie body was staggering listlessly as if it hadn't realized it was dead yet, the head simply gone in a mass of gray spray.

Finally I turned my sights on the son zombie. I worked the action, lined up my aim and pulled the trigger... just as he finally tripped and fell due to his jeans being around his ankles. I didn't know whether to laugh or be frustrated. In the end I chuckled to myself at how a "fashionable" teenager even made for an incompetent zombie. As I enjoyed that chuckle I worked the action to pump the next round into the chamber, took careful aim on the now belly-down and crawling zombie and fired. Due to the angle of impact, the zombie's head was pulped and pushed almost straight down its neck. As a result I actually saw the now headless torso expand with the pressure of it before collapsing back on its self, causing what had been the head and neck to come bubbling in a gray and white milky mess back out the neck hole. It was both disgusting and satisfactory to see at the same time.

I chambered the next round just to be ready, put the weapon on safe and slung it. The bodies still had to be stacked and burned, and no one was coming out to help me. Since the Chris zombie was the biggest, I stacked the others on top of him. First I scraped a small layer of magnesium shavings across him. Next I pulled the Shelby zombie over and laid her on top of him, as close to neatly stacked as I could manage, and then shaved some magnesium onto her as well. Next was the stupid teenager zombie body which I dragged by grabbing the jeans between his ankles and pulling. Disgustingly, both of his feet popped off at the ankles, apparently already sufficiently rotted that the jeans around his ankles while he walked had started to wear out the connection between leg and foot.

Controlling myself so as not to puke inside my protective mask, I threw the feet and jeans into the pile between the spread legs of Chris and Shelby. Then I pulled the stupid teenage zombie over by the wrists which thankfully didn't separate from the body. I put another layer of magnesium shavings on top of that one. Finally, had to put on the body of the nine-year-old little girl zombie. As a parent used to comforting children and mourning the loss of one so young,

I had the urge to pick up that small body and cradle it in my arms as I carried it over to its final resting place. Reality set in, though, and I knew that I didn't want to be that close to the thing. Grabbing her by an ankle, I pulled her over and put her on top of the pile.

From the container I'd brought out with me I doused the stack of bodies in about two gallons of gasoline and then stood back as I lit and threw a match. The first one went out before hitting, but the second one stayed lit and landed with a WHOOSH of igniting gasoline and fumes.

As the bodies burned, I looked around and saw faces in the windows of almost every house in the immediate vicinity. I knew what they were all thinking and feeling... and was quite happy not to be feeling it. None of them had it in them to come out and "kill" neighbors. Not even if the neighbors weren't human anymore; not even if the neighbors were zombies; not even if the zombies would quite happily kill and convert each of them and every member of their families.

While on the one hand, I felt like a complete monster because I was capable of this, on the other hand I knew I had only done what was necessary to protect my family and, in this case, the rest of my immediate neighborhood. I refused to feel guilty about that.

An hour later, I was inside and comfortable. My clothing had been disposed of appropriately. My shotgun had been cleaned and fully reloaded (having an unloaded gun around is as good as having a short hammer or club at hand). I had a cold beer in my hand and was waiting for my wife to finish making me a sandwich.

Was I a monster? I tried not to think about it. If I was, I was a live human monster and not a zombiefied walking dead monster. That would have to be good enough.

13

TRAVEL SAFETY

When traveling in or through any zombie-infested area, there are a number of considerations that need to be addressed. First and foremost, recognize that your vehicle is not a safe haven. While it will (temporarily) protect you from zombies, it will not do so indefinitely; when the time comes that it no longer offers protection, then it has merely become a cage with glass windows waiting to be broken out and reached into. And, for the love of all that's good, if you drive a convertible, trade it in now! Soft top Jeeps are ALMOST good to have because they often offer four-wheel drive capability and good off-road clearances. That said, the soft top is a detriment and needs to be avoided if at all possible.

Second, understand that your vehicle is not a permanent travel solution depending on the length of your trip. Anywhere along the way that vehicle can break down, and then your feet are your permanent travel solution. In any zombie infested area, whether you're in it or just passing through it, you must be prepared to leave your vehicle and travel on foot. That means you must have your survival necessities packed and with you in your vehicle *even if you're just going to the grocery store.*

"Survival necessities" are discussed in later chapters. For now let's review what the various pros and cons are of different vehicle types. The general rule of thumb is this: ***The bigger, the better.***

Four wheel drive vehicles rock. It's that simple. Why have only two wheels providing power from your drive train when you could have all four pushing and pulling? This may not seem to matter a lot, and, truth be told, many an auto buyer bought a four-wheel-drive vehicle that they never needed. Most front-wheel-drive vehicles will go through snow as well as four-wheel-drive (4x4) vehicles. Where most folks need 4x4 capability is off road, and, quite simply, most folks don't drive off road much. Welcome to a new reality.

Zombies, in case you hadn't realized, like to walk in the street as much as every ignorant pedestrian of the late 1990s. They don't obey crosswalks and would rather walk down nice wide roads and highways rather than shuffling along any sidewalk in a suburban neighborhood or city street. The result, unless you are supremely stupid and try to drive around them, is lots of speed bumps.

That said, it's important to realize that enough flattened zombies can add up to a substantial driving barrier. Four-wheel-drive capability and a strong enough motor/power train to get the weight of your vehicle up and over them are important. Otherwise the growing pile of zombies may be enough to eventually slow or stop your vehicle. Another rule of safety in a zombie-infested area: speed equals security. They move and react slow. If you move fast, it makes it harder for them to grab or hunt you.

So, 4x4 is required. Just accept it.

Four-by-fours come in a variety of sizes and shapes though. Let's start out with an examination of some big trucks. For decades the Army (and other services) have used the "deuce and a half" truck. This is a diesel powered ten-wheeled truck that is capable of hauling two and a half tons of equipment. That's five thousand pounds and is where the nickname "deuce and a half" came from: two and a half tons.

Some people make the mistake of thinking that various pickup trucks, such as the Dodge Ram 2500 or the Ford Super-Duty series carry the same amount. Don't make that mistake. There is a significant difference between a military purpose-built truck that is designed to carry 5,000 pounds and a truck that will carry a maximum of 2,500 pounds.

Realistically speaking, none of us will ever need to haul two and a half tons. Still, it's nice to have a structure with a drive train that will move that much weight, especially if you're in it and trying to drive through a hoard of fifty or more zombies. Even if each one only weighs 150 pounds, that's still over 7,500 pounds of zombie meat. No, you're not hauling it. No, you're not pushing it all (some is going under the truck). But you want to be able to push all you can so you don't slow down as much before they start falling down and end up pulped under your vehicle.

The other strength of bigger trucks is how high up the passenger compartment is. With a military deuce-and-a-half, you need a step ladder to get up in it OR you need to have the upper body strength to haul yourself up and in. That first step is about 2.5 or 3 feet off the ground, so zombies can't climb up onto it – at least not as far as anyone has ever observed. Trucks with high cabs share that strength.

Pickup trucks are great for storage capacity and the ability to put lifts in them, raising them to the require height to make sure zombies can't climb in. And, of course, you can get plenty of them with 4x4 drive capability. The challenge with many pickup trucks is their limited fuel efficiency. Not that a deuce-and-a-half gets great gas mileage, but it holds a LOT of diesel fuel. The average pickup truck holds about 25-30 gallons of gasoline, and after you've loaded it up with gear and are driving in four-wheel-drive, you get about 12 miles per gallon. All of a sudden that 25 gallons won't even carry you 300 miles. If that's your plan, then you need to consider auxiliary tanks and/or carrying plenty of gas cans.

You can also put a cap on the back of a pickup truck. If you do that, reinforce the cap's windows and add a layer of sealant between the cap and the rim around the truck bed. What you're trying to do is prevent air flow into the cap unless you open the windows. Be careful; on most caps, where the back window folds down to lock shut flush with the tailgate, there are gaps at both lower corners. Those gaps can usually be sealed with small pieces of self-adhesive foam strips that you can buy at any department store or sewing supply shop. Make sure the lock is strong, works easily (the last thing you want is to need something about of the back and you can't get to it in time because the lock sticks), and you have the key handy.

Of course, one solution to having a sealed cap is not to have a pickup truck but to have a "sport utility vehicle" (SUV) instead. With an SUV you essentially get an already enclosed pickup truck with nicer bed liner. Think about it. But it has to be a full-size SUV. Think Ford Expedition on steroids. Think Ford Excursion (if you can find one used since they went out of production early in the millennium). Think original ugly military production up-armored HMMWV (High Mobility Multipurpose Wheeled Vehicle – also commonly referred to as a "Humvee").

IF you're going to use an SUV as your vehicle in any zombie-infested area, you need, again, to make sure it sits high enough of the ground to avoid easy zombie reach or entrance through your windows. That's why the smaller SUVs aren't good as transport in such areas; if you put enough lift on them to get the windows high enough, because of their narrower width and lighter weight, they become unstable at speed.

Now some folks live and die by their four-door sedans. For decades, such vehicles were the primary patrol and response vehicles for law enforcement agencies all around the globe, and, therefore, people assumed they were the best vehicles to have if you had to go somewhere in a hurry. NOT! Think about it…

Moving around in the passenger compartment is difficult at best. Due to the limited roof clearance and smaller spaces between seats, especially if you're trying to switch positions without letting go of your long gun, it's difficult, if not downright dangerous. Further, if you *need* to access something in the trunk while you're moving, you are out of luck *unless* you have a split folding down rear seat that permits such access and you plan for that, storing your gear in the trunk accordingly.

There are also people who refuse to give up their sports cars. Their argument is that the pure speed and power of their small, two-door, close-to-the-ground, often-convertible car makes it the perfect zombie escape mobile. To those folks we say: Thank you for playing; enjoy your (however short lived) day.

This cannot be emphasized enough: your transport vehicle through any zombie-infested zone *must* have a hard top. It *must* sit at least ten inches off the ground (that's ground clearance, not door edge) and twelve to sixteen inches is preferred. It *must* weigh four thousand pounds or more, and it *must* have an engine capable of moving/pushing that four thousand pounds plus the weight of any zombies you run into, roll over, push, crush, etc.

Those same folks who claim that sports cars are the bomb thanks to their speed and mobility often also claim that the only thing better than a sports car is a motorcycle. We affectionately call these people "zombie appetizers." 'Nuff said.

So, after you've selected whatever vehicle you are going to use as your zombie zone transport, you need to properly prepare it as such. Primarily such customization requires adjustments to just a few things: the air intake system, the windows and the tires.

Let's start with the air intake system. Since the discovery of the fact that ingestion of even a single zombie virus particle will kill and convert you, everyone has paid a lot more attention to wearing protective masks and such. Then those same "wise" folks get in their car, turn their air conditioning on full blast and run over zombies, ignoring the potential for zombie goo to splatter into their air intake which will promptly push it through the fan and out the vents into the interior space of the car. There it gets inhaled by every occupant and, viola, instant car full of soon-to-be-zombies.

The first rule of zombie transport conversion: double filter the air coming into the vehicle, and, even then, ONLY use recirculated interior air flow if you have reason to suspect zombie goo on your vehicle's exterior anywhere.

The second rule is to mount air dams along the front, bottom and top edge of any window you think you might need to open while in motion. No, this will not stop air from coming into your vehicle through that open window; however, it will deflect, to some extent, any zombie goo that results from high-speed impact between your vehicle and any zombie in your path.

The third rule is to mount strong steel mesh over any window that you can without inhibiting your ability to open it. Yes, this is a "trade off" measure. It will protect you from zombies reaching through those windows. It also prevents you from escaping through those windows in the event of a vehicle accident. Recognize that life during a zombie outbreak is, in general, filled with risk and you have to reduce those risks sometimes by accepting other smaller risks. I'll risk being temporarily stuck in my vehicle after an accident if the window mesh prevents some zombie hoard from reaching in and yanking off the tasty morsels they call "ears."

Finally, purchase and mount "run flat" tires. These are tires specifically designed for law enforcement and military that allow the vehicle to continue moving at high speeds in controlled fashion even if one or more of the tires is punctured. They aren't cheap, but what's your life worth?

Those are the basic modifications that need to be made. There are other modifications you can make that will increase the effectiveness of your vehicle as a zombie transport/zombie cruncher.

A big wide and tall push bumper is a must. There are a number of variations, makes and models, but it's recommended that you mount one that is tilted away from your hood at the top. That way, when you run into zombies they are knocked down and under your vehicle and stand less chance of falling up and onto your hood – which leads to your windshield, through which is your passenger compartment. The last thing you want is splattered zombie goo all over the inside of your vehicle.

A good winch. If you get stuck, you can't count on anyone to come help you. Get a winch rated to pull the weight of your vehicle plus 1,000 pounds. That way if you get stuck the winch should be able to pull out your vehicle, even if it's full of gear.

🕱 **NOTE:** everyone traveling with you will likely have to get out of the vehicle if you have to winch it out of a spot. *Everyone* serves on perimeter security duty during such times. No exceptions; no excuses. If the person doesn't have a gun or has some moral compunction about shooting already dead but still homicidal zombies, why are they traveling with you in the first place? (Children too young to be taught to hold and shoot a gun exempted.)

Extra lights can come in handy; however, you don't want to mount a light bar in such a manner as to offer a hand-hold to any zombie or other bi-pedal predator (human). So, you mount the lights on the push bumper or on the A-pillar (that vertical side support for your windshield) of your vehicle. If you must put lights on top, make sure the mounting system is as low profile as it can be.

🕱 **NOTE:** It's been proven that flashing colored lights attract more attention from zombies than plain white lights. Don't mount surplus police or fire department light bars. Don't mount blue, green, orange or other neon light "accessories" on your vehicle. Avoid any colored light on your vehicle if you can. The red and amber lenses are still legally required in all fifty states even during zombie outbreaks so be aware of the legal risk you take if you modify them.

Finally, make sure you have at least one spare tire; two is better. Mount them on an equipment rack on top of your vehicle, but, again, make sure the rack mounts aren't easily grabbed by zombies (or anyone else). If they can be easily reached, consider welding or soldering razor blade halves onto the vertical uprights. That way if a zombie gets a hand hold they lose their fingers.

> **NOTE:** If you mount such "booby traps" on your vehicle, you may be held liable by your state and/or be in violation of the laws in some states. Be aware of your state statutes and in compliance with them.

With all of the above accomplished, you need to travel aware of the danger from flying zombie goo. Remember, it only takes a single zombie cell, *any* zombie cell, to infect you. You need to take the proper precautions to protect yourself and all passengers in your vehicle from airborne detritus.

Inside the vehicle, if the windows are open even the smallest amount, wear full wrap-around eye protection such as you would wear on the firing range or to perform surgery. The eyeball is one big wet sponge for flying zombie cells. Protect them.

If you're going to have those windows open even the least bit and you suspect for any reason that the area you're traveling in has experienced a zombie outbreak, wear painter's masks. Full protective masks are better, but at least a painter's mask (those light weight rubber-banded on white teardrop shaped things) will keep things from landing directly on your lips or nose, or worse, between your lips or up your nose.

All of this may seem quite paranoid and unnecessary. That's an easily held outlook until a member of your family gets zombiefied and tries to kill you. Don't go there. Take the necessary precautions.

14

WHEN WE ABANDONED OUR HOUSE & NEIGHBORHOOD

As dictated by Justin Rustovic and notated by Frank Borelli.

There came a point where my family and I had to leave our house. We didn't like the idea, but we'd reached an impasse. It was no longer safe to grocery shop in our immediate area, and the schools had been closed more often than not in the previous few months. Finally, we lived not too far from a nuclear power plant, and I was beginning to get concerned that it would be all too easy for the government to cover up a big zombie outbreak with a "nuclear accident" at the plant. If that happened, most of my county would be in trouble. It's not that big of a county, and if you take out three bridges, it's more of an island than a peninsula. I don't own a boat, so if we were going to go, we needed to go before anything ugly happened to the bridges.

My wife and I had talked and agreed. As part of our zombie preparation, we had been keeping "go-bags" packed and ready for years. There was one go-bag for each person in the family.

Each go-bag held the basic necessities of life such as a change of clothes, medicines for the particular individual the go-bag was designed for, miscellaneous survival supplies, etc. My family consists of me, my wife, my sixteen-year-old son, my twelve-year-old son, and my eight-year-old daughter. Five people total. None of us had any serious health concerns. My teenagers were amazingly mature in their behavior given the situation.

In addition to the go-bags we also had a container stocked and ready to go with basic survival necessities for the family. We had a plan in place. We were going to pack our truck and head for her family's farm in Utah. The Midwest was much safer than anywhere east of the Mississippi River simply because the population was far less dense. Having the population more spread out meant less infection from a single zombie... and let's be honest: the folks out west are used to fending for themselves. Everybody and their brother carries a gun and knows how to shoot. If a zombie strolls down the street, five or six people will, without causing a cross-fire, pull out a handgun of respectable caliber and shoot it in the head. Minutes thereafter, someone will douse the gray corpse in gasoline and torch it.

So, our plan was to head west. Our truck was prepared. The truck itself is a four-wheel drive Dodge Ram 2500 that had been customized for the intended use. None of the customized features LOOKED custom. From a casual look, all you'd see is a Dodge Ram 2500 with a cap over the bed. The cap had limo-black tinted windows on the sides and clear windows in the top. The clear top windows had steel mesh mounted over them with a steel framework that held them into place.

I had a few spare parts and enough oil, along with the requisite filters, to make three oil changes. I had two one-hundred gallon gas storage tanks custom built into the sideboards of the bed of the truck so we had over two hundred gallons of gas. At an average travel rate of approximately 350 miles per 25-gallon tank of gas, we had enough gas to travel over 2,500 miles. Since that's the country's width coast-to-coast, and since I expected to be able to buy gas normally as we traveled, I felt like we had more than enough.

Into the covered truck bed went our necessities kit which held an eight-person cabin-type tent (bigger than we needed), six all-weather sleeping bags (one more than we needed), miscellaneous cooking needs (pots, pans, utensils, cleaning stuff, plates, cups, etc.), four crates of food – none of which required refrigeration – and fifty gallons of fresh water in sealed containers. With the water we included two filter systems that would allow us to filter as much as another two thousand gallons of water if needed. We also had eight gallons of bleach that were loaded into crates and a pump-pressure delivery system similar to the ones used by pest-control workers. You put in your liquid, pump it up and push the nozzle release. You can set it to a fine spray or a mist, and we intended to use it to spray bleach around any camping areas we used along the way. The go-bags also went into the truck bed.

Into the cab of the truck with us went six protective masks (normally called "gas masks" – one more than we needed), four rifles (one for each person except my daughter), five handguns (one for each person), extra ammo for everyone, and six sets of protective eyewear. We also had two packages of breathing filters of the type painters wear when they are spraying paint.

They didn't seal out contamination, but they reduced the amount of unfiltered air you might inhale.

We didn't know how long the trip west would take us, but we had planned the route, marked our intended camping spots and were underway. Everyone knew their jobs and responsibilities. We had a full family brief on the location of equipment prior to leaving. Our immediate area had suffered a zombie outbreak less than three days earlier, so we agreed to travel with the windows closed and the air system turned off. Our intention was to travel at least thirty miles before cracking the windows. When we did, we knew we'd all enjoy the fresh air, but we also knew we'd all be putting on the protective eyewear and painter's masks. It was a tossup, but by then we were sure we'd all want some fresh air flow.

Traveling north out of our neighborhood we fully realized that we might see a zombie, or a few, along the way. We weren't worried. We were properly prepared and no zombie in the history of zombies (over 60,000 years now if you were a good student of them) had ever been seen running, much less running fast enough to keep up with a motorized vehicle. In addition, as described earlier, our truck was built up specifically to be used as a zombie-crushing machine if need be.

What I didn't expect was what we found. Once we got out of our neighborhood we were about an hour's drive south of the nearest big city. Long before we got close I had planned to turn west. I could have started out going south and then hooked west, but the highway layout made initial northward travel more favorable. The highways were wider, and immediately north of us is less densely populated than immediately south of us. Everything made sense for us to start out north, travel about twenty minutes and then make our turn west. We'd have to travel over a two-lane bridge, but we'd have to do that sooner or later anyway. Our county is pretty much a peninsula so bridges are a reality. Lately I'd found myself pondering the wisdom of moving to a small island but that's a different challenge.

So, there we were heading north and we'd been on the road for about ten minutes. As I mentioned earlier, our area is still pretty well populated by Amish folks. Their farms are scattered across the landscape around us, and since they loath technology of any kind, they were more susceptible than the rest of us to zombie infection.

The most recent outbreak in our area, as I said, had been about three days prior, and we were pretty confident that it had spread as far as it was going to. Once news of any outbreak spread, people acted accordingly and the outbreak got squashed pretty quick. The government never investigated zombie destructions beyond sending CDC representatives to make sure the body disposal was handled properly. There were just too many outbreaks for them to do much else.

As we drove up the road, our assumption was that anyone who was going to change had changed and any zombie we came across would be pretty much a loner. Little did we know.

About ten minutes up the road we found ourselves in the middle of a cluster of Amish farms and we were totally surprised to see a whole field full of zombie cows. Who ever heard of a zombie cow? Much less a herd of them? It was so weird we had to slow down and look. That was all it took to attract their attention though. As we slowed down, every bovine head turned our way, almost as if moved by the same muscle. The lowing that came out of these animals almost sounded like their normal mooing but it had an edge to it that sounded different.

I put my foot back down on the accelerator but got concerned when I saw more of the same herd farther up the road… in the middle of the road. Now my truck might have done just fine against twenty or thirty "human" zombies, but fifty or sixty cow zombies? I knew we couldn't push that weight and I wondered what our next step was.

As I thought, I realized that the road had no borders or restrictions to keep me on it. I could drive the shoulder or surrounding fields. It was one of the reasons most of the locals hated this stretch of road, even pre-outbreak: the farmers didn't put up fences, and traffic was often interrupted by cows in the road. That same lack of fencing that let the cows get into the road would also let me get off the road. My challenge was going to be finding a break in this heard of zombie cows. How ridiculous could things get?

My son asked me if we should shoot the cows. I told him not to waste the bullets. I'm sure it had happened somewhere at some point, but I'd never heard of anyone being bitten by a cow. And these particular cows didn't seem anything more than curious about our presence. Did they crave other cow brains? Other cow flesh?

Many of them showed marks on their bodies where it looked like they'd been scratched or cut. Nothing I could see when I slowed down to navigate between the larger bunches looked like a bite mark. There finally came a point where I had to get off the road to go around a group of about a dozen or so of them, and as soon as I found my break in the mass of cows I accelerated into it… never expecting a human zombie to jump (well, kind of jump) out from between some of the cows.

Our push bumper impacted him pretty hard since I was still going about forty miles per hour. I was pretty sure he couldn't smell us but was reacting to the truck itself. After all, if zombies could hunt then they could also, somehow, understand that only healthy humans drove vehicles.

Upon impact, his body fell down and rolled under the truck's bumper. His head did not. Separated from the body pretty neatly at the neck, the head bounced over the hood, left a greenish-white gooey smear on the windshield and then bounced up and over the roof. We heard it thump once on the bed cap and then it was gone. In the side view mirror I saw what was left of the zombie body on the ground behind us. Admittedly zombies usually look pretty nasty anyway, but this body was chewed up pretty well. I guess the various edges and pieces of a vehicle undercarriage as it tumbles you along will do that.

The body didn't get up, or make any attempt that I saw. They'll sometimes do that even though it defies all laws of logic. The cows, on the other hand, reacted in a completely unexpected fashion: they began to spread out away from the mutilated zombie body. It was almost as if they didn't like the smell, which made no sense at all. I wasn't about to complain though. Apparently the greenish-white smear on the windshield had the same effect on them; or maybe it was the smear of flesh under the truck? Whatever it was, the cows began to spread out in front of me, leaving me a clear path of travel. I found myself wondering if there were any other zombies around I could hit or run over.

Once we were clear of the zombie cow herd, we got back on the highway and continued our travel. After having experienced something so weird I was thinking that we'd run into no more surprises. We only had another twelve to fifteen miles to go and then we'd be turning west and clear of most of the local dangerous areas. It was only about three miles later that we ran into our challenge.

Several zombies were walking in the road; not traveling in any particular direction but just wandering around. It looked like each time one would get close to the edge of the pavement it would turn and walk in a different direction just to stay on the pavement. All of them were dressed in suits which made no sense to me, but didn't make any difference either. Well-dressed zombies were still just zombies and the only real question that existed was how to destroy them most efficiently.

In this case I didn't have to slow down much but was able to avoid them. We crested a small hill and found the answer to our question of where the well-dressed zombies had come from: a commuter bus was wrecked on the side of the road. It looked like it had run into a state highway maintenance truck that had been stopped for whatever reason. Maybe the crew had been picking up trash. After all, the way governments work, no matter what else might be going on, the trivial stuff still has to be accomplished.

Apparently there was someone infected on board the bus, or maybe multiple someones. The bus looked like it would hold about 80 passengers and I guessed that to be about how many zombies were wandering around. Idly I wondered what their hesitation was about stepping off the roadway, but honestly I didn't care. Unless they became a problem, I had no intention of stopping. None of them had seemed to notice us and I wasn't slowing down. Then Mr. Murphy, of Murphy's Law (anything that can go wrong will go wrong) paid us a visit. Something under the hood popped and steam began whistling out from the engine compartment. Almost at the same moment the temperature gauge for the motor started to climb and I knew I wasn't going to drive a lot further.

Something I had learned as a child bubbled up from my memory, but I didn't think it was a tactic that would be smart to use given the circumstances. I had learned that if an engine is overheating you can help cool it down by turning on your vehicle's heat and opening all the windows so you don't get cooked. This provided some air movement over the motor which helped to keep it from overheating as fast; however, in our circumstance, we didn't want potentially infected air being sucked in through the ventilation system, nor did we want it blowing in through open windows. As a result, we were left with few options.

With an overheating engine that I couldn't cool down and several dozen zombies in the immediate area, I tried to figure out how far I could drive before we had to abandon the truck. Making matters worse was the fact that, for whatever reason, the steam from the truck had attracted the attention of some of the closer zombies. They began turning to wander toward us, even as we continued to drive, and their change in behavior seemed to prompt a change in the behavior of the others. The next thing I knew we had better than two dozen zombies following the slowly dying truck. Good news for us: we were still traveling in excess of forty miles per hour. Bad news for us: at some point we'd have to bail out and we didn't want to do it into a hoard of zombies.

Before it totally seized up, I was able to drive the truck about another five miles. That put plenty of space between us and the zombies and even more between us and the herd of zombie cows. (The weirdness of that was still fresh in my mind.) We "dismounted" from the truck, grabbed our go-bags and weapons and started out.

Almost immediately we were set upon by three zombies. The oddest part was that one was a deputy sheriff, one was what looked like a fireman (blue uniform and Maltese cross badge/ patch), and the last one looked like a tow truck driver. Even as we were dealing with the threat I was trying to figure out how these three ended up wandering together.

I didn't ponder that long; at least not long enough to distract me from doing what needed done. Raising my rifle, I fired a .30-.30 caliber round into the face of the one closest to me – the fireman zombie. I heard my wife trigger off a round from her shotgun and looked over in time to see the tow truck driver zombie's head evaporate into a cloud of greenish-white goo (it kind of looked like rotten tapioca pudding). My oldest son didn't hesitate to get in the fight either. I heard his rifle fire, and when I looked over, I could see where his first shot had been just a little low, going through the throat of the deputy sheriff zombie instead of its head. My son adjusted quickly and fired his second round, a nice neat little hole appearing just below the zombie's left eye. Less than a blink of a moment thereafter a baseball sized chunk of yuck blasted away from the back of the zombie's head. It was weird to see the zombie stand there for a few seconds, his milky white eyes looking even more distant and empty than usual. And then he fell over like a tree that had been cut down – slowly and almost perfectly straight, as if he was stiff for some reason.

We moved away from that area quickly, and as we traveled I had a thought connected to the stiff falling zombie: when a person dies and prior to starting their transition into a zombie, did rigor mortis ever set in? It was something to study when the opportunity presented itself, although, truth be told, I'd be perfectly happy not to ever have the chance to find out.

15

TRAVELING ON FOOT SURVIVAL CONCERNS

Obviously, when you're traveling on foot in any area that is zombie infested, or has recently experienced a zombie outbreak, there are a number of concerns that need to be addressed. The first is our own personal physical fitness.

Understand this because it is vitally important: *out of shape people are zombie snacks.* Zombies don't get tired. Zombies don't get fatigued. Zombies don't stop to rest, and they never sleep. Zombies never get full. Just because they finished snacking on ten of your best friends *does not* mean they aren't still coming for you. Once transformed, zombies keep chasing food (that would be us for those of you not keeping up) until their muscles atrophy to the point of failure.

Therefore it's important that we increase our own levels of endurance to the highest level we are individually capable of. Once the fight with zombies is engaged, it's not over until the last zombie has been put down. Quitting the fight before that means succumbing to becoming the main course in the zombie feast.

The second consideration, just as obviously, is survival. Not only do we need to carry our weapons and ammo, but we also need to carry all of our other supplies. Due to the limited space available, even if we use the largest backpack available, the comfort levels experienced are a far cry different from those we are typically used to. In addition to maximizing your own levels of physical fitness and endurance, you must also streamline what supplies you carry. The balance to be found is: sufficient and necessary supplies to survive but not so much gear that it prevents you from moving faster and longer than the nearest zombie hoard.

Additionally, whereas on a recreational backpacking trip you don't have to carry weapons and ammo, you absolutely must if you're traveling in a zombie-infested or potentially zombie-infested area. And, since you never quite know where your travel plans will be affected or redirected by zombies, you can't plan for a specific timeline. Once you're on foot, you must accept the reality that you are potentially traveling on foot with sporadic rest for the rest of your life. That "rest of your life" is only as long as you can outrun and/or regularly stop any zombies you encounter.

The third consideration is constant and perpetual perimeter security. Even when you are moving, you must maintain an awareness of any and every potential threat that exists around you for as far as you can see or hear. It is difficult, at best, for a lone traveler to provide for his (or her) own 360° security. That's why it is best to travel in teams. Many folks find themselves traveling in family packs, and there are pros as well as cons to that reality.

A family traveling together has an unspoken deep commitment to the survival of each family member. The chances that a family member will take in an effort to save another family member are often much greater than those accepted by unrelated team members. That group drive to survive is a positive factor that often tips the balance of group survival in a positive fashion.

On the other hand, if a family member is lost or killed or, even worse, transformed into a zombie, it is quite demoralizing to the rest of the family. Unless that family has a strong leader with a well-anchored grasp of reality who can drive that family on to survival in spite of the loss or transformation of a family member, then the whole family can be lost.

If you are traveling in a non-family-unit team, the reality is different. The team functions together to increase the overall chance of survival for everyone in the team; however, if a team member is lost, killed, or transformed, the cold harsh reality of continuing on without a lot of mourning is easier to accept.

The important point here, though, is that no matter whether you travel in a family team or a non-related team, the 360° security has to be maintained both while you're moving and while you're at rest. This requires predetermined responsibilities. The team leader, whether formally delineated or not, is responsible for perimeter assignments.

The most commonly used formations for movement include the diamond and the modified cigar. Both are taken from the law enforcement and military communities. The typical diamond formation was developed to incorporate each member of a four-man "fire team." Most military squads have nine members, including the squad leader, so 2 four-man fire teams provide an assignment or responsibility for each squad member. That just leaves the squad leader, and he falls into one or the other diamond making it a five-man diamond formation. Remember this: *nothing is written in stone.* Use all of this information as best you can and modify it or customize it to suit your needs.

The diamond formation uses either four or five people and looks (roughly) something like this:

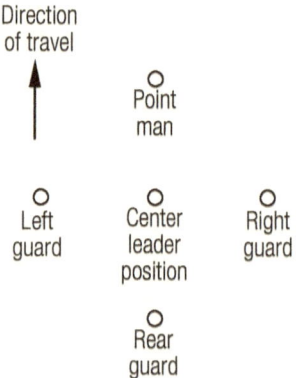

If the diamond formation is used for five people, then typically the team leader will assume a central position in the middle of the diamond. In doing so, he can communicate easily with all four "diamond points," and he is properly positioned to step into and assume a diamond point position should any of the team members fall for any reason.

In using the diamond formation, it's necessary for every team member to understand that the rear guard has the hardest job. It's quite impossible (without tons of training time and even then only on perfectly smooth terrain) to walk backwards and stay with the group. That means the rear guard has to walk in the same direction and at the same pace as the team but must also constantly be checking the 90° space behind the team. The left guard is responsible for the 90° to the left; the right guard is responsible for the 90° to the right; the point man is responsible for the 90° to the front. Four 90° angles added together equals 360° coverage.

Due to basic body mechanics, if there's a left-handed shooter in your team, he's best positioned at right guard; that way his weapon is comfortably pointed in the correct direction as you travel. (All guns should be pointed out of the diamond formation as a matter of safe practice.)

The final note on using the diamond formation is that responsibilities can change dependent on the situation and direction of travel. In the diagramed formation, the direction of travel shown is straight ahead (up the page). If that team were to turn left, then the responsibilities would change. The diamond would not curve around so that the point man stayed point man; right guard stayed right guard, etc. Doing so is not efficient, and anything that costs time in a combat/survival situation is not good. So, instead, the team members simply turn left, stay in relative position to each other, and assume new responsibilities based on their position relative to their direction of travel.

 NOTE: remember your muzzle discipline – *do not point your weapon at your team member!*

Example:

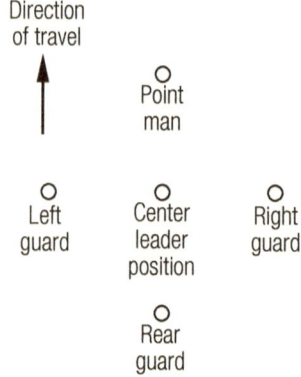

Then the team makes a left turn:

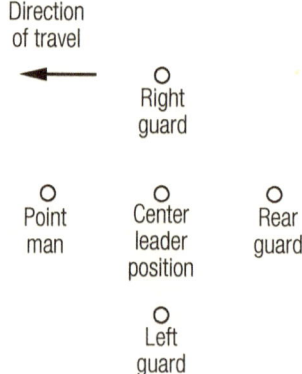

The rear guard's focus of attention is always the opposite direction as that of the team's movement.

Another note on using the diamond formation: as mentioned, quite often the team leader is in the middle of the diamond if there is a five-person team; however, if you have a "weak" member of your team – someone who isn't a great shot or who is low on ammo as examples – you can put them in the middle of the diamond. This serves two purposes: first, it protects them; second, it keeps the strongest perimeter possible in place. If you are a family group moving in the diamond formation, this strategy can be used to put the youngest (and typically weakest) member of your family in the middle – the most guarded position.

The other commonly used travel formation, usually used when there are six or more team members, is the "modified cigar" formation. The modified cigar can be used fluidly to suit various sized teams.

Using the example of seven team members, the formation looks something like this:

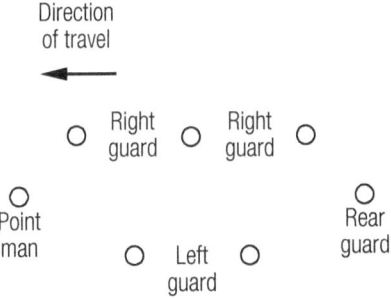

If you had eight members, one more would be added to the left side of the formation. Common sense dictates that members on the right side are responsible for security on the right; members on the left are responsible for security on the left. The point man and rear guard responsibilities don't change.

Another option if you have eight or nine (or ten) team members is to break into two groups (military term "fire team") and have two diamonds moving independently but in a coordinated fashion. Using two teams, when you have enough members, gives you the strength of minimizing risk. If you're moving into an area where there is an unknown risk or you have a confirmed but unmeasured risk, you can move one team ahead while holding one team back, thereby risking only half your members. While such a tactic may seem cold or callous, it is a proven combat survival tactic.

Standard infantry tactics mandate a space of approximately three meters (ten feet) between each member. That keeps the team spaced out which makes them harder to kill with a single machine gun burst, a single grenade, or all in an ambush at the same time; however, that tactic does not apply when operating in a zombie-infested environment. While it's necessary to maintain sufficient space to fight efficiently, since zombies don't use weapons, such a wide spacing is not required. One to two meters between team members is the recommended spacing.

The more people there are in your movement formation, the more aware everyone needs to be aware of weapons discipline, especially when engaging active zombies. It is all too easy if a single team member panics to shoot other team members if you're not paying careful attention to your fields of fire. NEVER index (point your weapon at) another team member.

Perimeter security is not only important during movement. Your team must be mindful of any threat from any direction whether you are mobile or not. In fact, movement itself offers some level of security. "Speed is security" is an old infantry axiom, and where zombies are concerned, it is definitely true. It's EASY to outrun zombies if you stay on your feet, think ahead and don't run into a corner. The challenge we face is that zombies don't sleep and don't get tired. We do. So when the time comes that we need to rest and are in a secure enough position to do so, perimeter security is all the more important because we are not only in a static (not moving) position but also asleep.

Two standard operating procedures/rules for resting/sleeping in a zombie-infested or suspected zombie occupied area:

1) One fourth of your team always stays awake and alert.

2) Caffeine and sugar are your friend for up to 48 hours.

"One fourth" of the team is defined as exactly that: ¼ of your operational team members but NEVER less than TWO. If your team is five people, two stay awake while others sleep. The watch gets traded off as necessary. Understand that up to ten people only means two people staying awake at a time (mandated – more is optional). Once you reach a team size of more than ten (11-15), then you should have three team members awake. Sixteen to nineteen people get four people staying awake, etc.

While everyone who is tired wants to sleep, no one wants to get dead or transformed either. The more people who stay awake, the less responsibility each watchman has and the more guns are available in the event that zombies find your team.

In the event zombies find your team, everyone wakes up to fight (usually to the sound of gunfire), and then your entire team must decamp and move immediately following the engagement. Once a campsite has been identified by even a single zombie, it can no longer be considered safe.

While it has been discovered that burning a zombie body will keep zombies away from a particular area for a brief period of time, it's also been discovered (the hard way) that this works less efficiently in rural areas. There seems to be some connection between population density, how built up an area is, and the burning of a zombie body. Lower population densities and more rural spaces seem to have a diluting effect of the burned zombies on the still mobile ones.

For maximum security, your perimeter should be set out at least five meters from your camp. The more people you can put on perimeter, the farther out you can and should push it. For example, if you have a party of five, that means two guards are awake while three members sleep. With the camp in the middle, the guards would be positioned approximately ten meters apart – about five meters from the center of the camp directly opposite from each other on either side of the camp.

Second example: if you have a party of twenty, keeping the sleeping members relatively tight in the camp, at least five guards are spread out around the camp approximately seven to eight meters out from the center of the camp. This affords more space inside the perimeter for the camp itself as well as a greater gap between the guards and the campers which is good in the event any zombies actually approach the camp. The farther away from the center of the camp the first engagement occurs, the more reaction time the team members have to ready a full response.

16

WHEN OUR TRUCK
BROKE DOWN

As dictated by Justin Rustovic and notated by Frank Borelli.

We organized ourselves into a five-man diamond and began to move. As we moved, I considered our strengths and weaknesses, our weapons, and our tactics. We had a general direction of travel in mind, but we hadn't planned on traveling so far on foot to get to our destination. What I needed was some place I could secure my family and some time to go back to the truck to repair it. I knew all too well that traveling on foot for long periods of time in any zombie-outbreak or zombie-infested area eventually meant two things:

1) Running out of ammo, and/or

2) Potentially having to fight past exhaustion.

So, as we walked I took mental stock. I was on point. As the leader of the family, I should probably have been in the middle position, but our weakest family member was there, protected and buffered from any zombies we might encounter. I was armed with my Winchester lever-action .30-.30 rifle and had about fifty rounds of ammo for it on my person. I also had my Springfield Armory Government Model 1911 pistol and six loaded 8-round magazines for it in addition to the one that was in it. For cutting weapons, I had a KA-BAR ZK War Sword and a ZK Famine Tanto. The "ZK" stood for "Zombie Killer." KA-BAR had started the line during the zombie craze before the reality of zombie outbreaks was made public. They never stopped making the edged weapons, and I'm pretty sure they sold even more after the reality of zombies was admitted by our world's governments. I also had a Tomahawk, a "Hawkspike" designed and manufactured by K5 Tactical, but it was mounted to my pack and would take forever for me to deploy. It was, for all intents and purposes, useless as a weapon unless it was already in my hand when an attack came, and then it would be an awesome weapon. The front was like any other axe, but the back edge was a spike designed to punch through sheet-steel walls. That it would punch through a zombie cranium and destroy massive amounts of brain tissue went without saying.

My wife, Dana, was walking rear guard with her Remington 870 shotgun. It was loaded to capacity with the previously described PolyShok ammo, and she had a mix of twelve gauge slugs and 00 buck in a side-saddle shell holder. On her left thigh, she had a rig that carried another 36 rounds of ammo for the shotgun. On her right thigh was her Glock Model 17 9mm handgun. She had six magazines full of ammo for it plus the one in it. In this case, "full" meant 19 rounds per magazine. They normally hold 17 rounds a piece, but we had put on "+2" floorplates which increased the capacity of each to 19. So she had eight rounds of twelve gauge immediately available in the shotgun and 20 rounds of 9mm in her handgun. Additionally she had two knives just like I did. In fact, she had the same set: a KA-BAR ZK War Sword and a ZK Famine Tanto. We both carried the War Sword on our left hip, but I carried the Famine Tanto on my vest – right in the center of my chest so I could reach it with either hand – while she carried her Famine Tanto on her belt above her handgun at her right hip.

On the right side of the diamond was my oldest son Nathan, affectionately called "Nate." He was armed with a Del-Ton AR-15 chambered for .223. Although I wasn't excited about the stopping power of the cartridge, he had proven competent with the weapon, and it was what we had available for him. He had seven 30-round magazines for it, one of which was loaded into the weapon. The other six he carried on a chest rig. His handgun was a Glock Model 19 9mm and he had seven magazines for that as well. Normally holding fifteen rounds each, we had changed the floorplates out on his magazines as well so that they each held seventeen rounds. He carried them in pouches on his belt and on the chest rig he wore. He had a regular machete at his left hip and a KA-BAR D2 Extreme combat knife just behind the gun on his right side.

On the left side of the formation was my next son, twelve year old Jonathan, or "Johnny," for short. Johnny had hit his first growth spurt the year before, so he was about five feet four inches tall; big enough, at any rate, to carry a Del-ton AR-15 identical to the one Nathan had. Instead of six extra magazines, he only had four. His handgun was a Sig Sauer P226 9mm. He had three 15-round magazines for it. The two spares he carried on his belt. He only carried one knife, and it was the KA-BAR Combat Tanto which he positioned on his left hip.

On a semi-ironic semi-humorous note, both of their AR rifles were equipped with a "Zombie Stopper" site manufactured by EOTech. The holographic site had been around for about a decade, but when the zombie craze set in, EOTech, like many others, climbed on board and made a zombie-specific product: The Zombie Stopper site. What made it different from their other sites was the reticle design. Instead of using a standard dot-in-the-middle-of-a-circle reticle, they used a modified HAZMAT symbol. Once the reality of zombie outbreaks was public knowledge, the entire industry had to acknowledge the forethought displayed by EOTech. Zombies were indeed a biohazard and their bodies a HAZMAT threat. Few others made that connection prior to the public dissemination of such by the government.

In the middle of our formation was my daughter, Ashley, all of eight years old. In her hands she carried an FNH 5.7mm handgun. Carrying 21 rounds of 5.7mm ammo, the weapon recoiled lightly so it was easy for her to handle. That said, the grips were a bit long, front to back, for her small hands. She had four magazines for it total and could perform reloads pretty quickly. She carried the weapon with the manual safety on. I had mixed feelings about that but ultimately decided it was safest given her central position in our travel formation. She, too, had a knife – a standard USMC issue KA-BAR combat knife in a leather sheath.

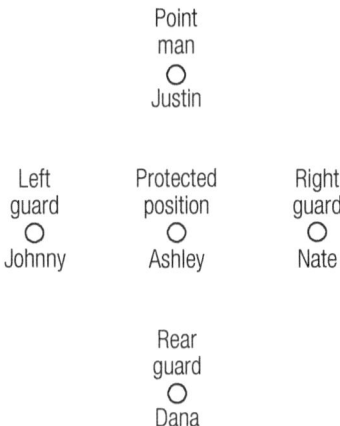

In addition to all our weapons, each of us was carrying our own go-bag, and each go-bag had a hydration system incorporated into it. Each hydration system held slightly less than one gallon of clean water (three liters), and each of us had an in-line filter we could use with our hydration systems if we found ourselves in the unenviable position of having to use water we found along the way.

Johnny's pack also had a Tactical Tomahawk from K5 Tactical strapped to the side. I had seen him use it in practice on pineapples and coconuts, and I was confident he could easily split a zombie's head open with it if need be. His challenge, like mine, would be deploying it quickly. Primarily he carried it to chop firewood and any sticks we needed to make shelters when we camped.

Every pack had a ration of food and some first aid supplies as well. Each pack had the necessary items to construct/erect basic shelters to protect us from wind and rain but wouldn't do much to protect us from cold temperatures. To help keep us warm, each pack included an Emergency Survival Bivvy from Adventure Medical Kits (AMK). The bivvy was essentially a light-weight insulated sleeping bag that used space-age materials to retain body heat.

Each of us had two flashlights, and we all had spare batteries for them as well. Were the loads light? No. Were we carrying anything but absolute essentials? No. None of my family members complained. In fact, we didn't talk at all as we walked along. There was about five feet between me and Nate; about five feet between me and Johnny; about three feet between me and Ashley (she liked to follow me close) and about ten feet between Dana and I. Idly I thought about how Dana's neck would be sore the next day from moving her head back and forth so much, but there was nothing to be done about it. That was the rear guard's job. When we took a rest break she could switch out with Nate if she wanted to give her neck a rest.

We didn't talk because sound can carry a long way, and we knew zombies could hunt us not only by smell but by sound as well. We did our best not to stir up the ground too much as we walked because we didn't want to leave a scent trail. Darling little Ashley had a runny nose, and I knew Dana would complain about the collection of snot on Ashley's sleeve later. It was an odd thought to have as I silently thanked God for my daughter being disciplined enough not to sniff to clear her nose; she simply wiped it on her sleeve.

Our plan, hastily conceived and communicated as we loaded up and left the truck, was to walk westward into the next county and stop at the house of a friend of ours. I had called him on my cell phone, which still (miraculously) worked, but he wouldn't come out to get us. His concern was the bridge connecting our county to his county. It was my concern too.

About seven miles away (if we'd been driving still), the bridge was only one lane in either direction. I had felt confident that we could get across it without incident in our truck because, quite frankly, zombies weren't going to slow down the momentum and inertia of a three ton vehicle going seventy-plus miles per hour. Of course, I hadn't planned on a popped hose causing the truck to break down either.

The reality we were now facing was a seven-mile hike just to get to the bridge and then getting across the bridge. Just like in a combat zone, such a narrow span is a higher risk for travelers. Not only does it mean that fewer zombies can block your direction of travel, but it also gives still-human criminal predators an easier place to target victims. Again, 70 mph in the truck makes us harder to slow down or hurt. On foot would be a different risk altogether. But we had little choice. Our other option was to walk back home, and that was even farther away than my buddy's house across the bridge.

We also knew, given the time of day and the fact that our pace would be set by our slowest family member (Ashley, with the shortest legs), there was no way we were going to get across the bridge before dark. We'd have to get as far as we could and set up camp. I knew there was a park with baseball fields within a mile of the bridge, and I felt that camping in the middle of one of the fields would be a good idea. That way we had plenty of visibility all around to more easily see what might be coming our way.

So with our basic plan laid out, we shouldered our packs, grabbed our weapons, locked the truck and headed west. We barely got a mile down the road before we ran into our first zombie challenge.

The area we had to walk through was almost one hundred percent Amish farmland. This was both a good and bad thing. For whatever sociological reason, populations like the Amish, who spurned technology, seemed to have a higher infection and conversion rate to zombieism. That was the bad part. The good part is that Amish farms don't have a high density of population. For about every one hundred acres of farm you might have four to ten people, two to eight of them children of varying ages.

So, although we had about seven miles to walk until we got to the bridge, most of it was Amish farmland and the rest was a state park. State parks were also pretty safe because anyone who turned zombie in the park almost always wandered out of the park in search of human meat.

The first mile we walked was all Amish farmland; pastures, barns, hay fields and the like. We passed two zombie cows that were so atrophied they couldn't even moo at us as we passed by, but we could feel their milky gray eyes staring at us. We all had on our protective eyewear and painter's masks. I knew that we'd be safer from protection if we wore our protective (gas) masks, but if you've never done it you can't really appreciate how uncomfortable it is. As a result of only wearing the painter's masks, we could also smell the rotten corpse stench of the cows. Yuck. It seems weird to say or think, but we were thankful for the fact that we'd smelled enough rotting zombie corpses – even the animated ones – that we'd grown somewhat used to the smell of rotting flesh. It still stank, but didn't make any of us gag like it used to.

We were moving in our diamond formation, our weapons held relaxed but ready. Everyone's finger was off the trigger, and every safety was on. The last thing any of us wanted to have happen was for one of us to trip and negligently pull a trigger. We had just passed the two zombie cow corpses and gone around a barn, leaving plenty of space between us and it, when four zombies came out of the barn behind us.

In the rear guard position, Dana saw them first. She shouted one word, "Contact rear!" immediately followed by the loud boom of the shotgun. I turned just in time to see a zombie head disintegrate in a cloud of gray mist. From the looks of the clothing it was an adult Amish male. The other three zombies were all smaller, looking like an adult female (in one of those beige dresses with light blue flowers on it) and two teenage boys (based on their size).

Seeing both Nate and Johnny turn to join the engagement, I turned back to the front. With the zombie threat to our rear (as delineated by our direction of travel), I still had responsibility for our safety from the opposite direction – our front. As I turned back around to "the front," I brought my rifle up into alignment with my line of sight, my thumb cocking back the hammer. I kept my finger off the trigger but swiveled my head, with the rifle kept in line with my vision, looking for any threat. My upper body resembled a tank turret with the gun turning in every direction I looked.

Behind me I heard Dana's shotgun boom again and the action working. I heard Nate's and Johnny's AR-15s both bark twice each and subconsciously counted off five shots. I felt movement at my right leg and glanced down to see Ashley on one knee beside me, almost using me as a barricade for support or cover. Her body language might have been timid but her eyes were searching in the same direction as mine and her pistol was up level in her line of sight, safety on, trigger finger lined up alongside the frame.

With my ears still ringing from the blasts of all three weapons I could barely hear Dana say, "Clear!" Nate and Johnny both echoed her word, thereby letting Ashley and I know that the threat had been defeated. For another few seconds we all held our positions, and then the boys moved turned back to face front with their eyes searching their designated areas of responsibility.

"Reload before we move," I commanded. The boys may have only spent a couple rounds each out of their magazines, but you just never knew when you'd need every bullet you had. Besides, it was a lesson Travis had pounded into our training regimen: always reload immediately upon having fired any rounds – as soon as you safely could.

As I kept my eyes searching in front of us, I heard Dana shoving twelve gauge rounds into the tubular magazine of the shotgun at the same time I heard the boys eject the magazines from their rifles and new ones being slammed home. Both guns already had rounds chambered so I didn't hear the charging handles pulled or released.

My ears registered those sounds as my eyes searched in front of us. There were two farm houses I could see; one several hundred yards away and the other even farther away past that. There were also two barns and an assortment of what looked like stables. One of the barns was about the same distance from us as the farm house was and on its south side. We'd walk a wide berth around each structure, thereby allowing ourselves as much reaction time as possible for any threat that might emerge from within any one of them.

Behind me I heard, "Ready!" chorused three separate times. It was the delineated way of them letting me (and Ashley) know that they were topped off on ammo and ready to move out.

"Moving," I said and began to walk again. I was leading us on a path that would take us around the north side of the nearest farm house. Looking at the way the structures were placed I felt that going north around, and giving a wide berth to, the house would be our safest route of travel, plus it kept us from going in between the house and one barn.

It was inevitable that our path of travel would, at some point, put the house in our line of site to one or more of the other structures. We'd lose sight of them, for whatever brief period of time it took us to move far enough along that we saw them around the house again. None of us was prepared for what we ran into.

As we reached the apex of our curve around the house, we were taken by surprise by five zombies that came out of the back door. "Contact left!" yelled Johnny on my left side. I turned, as did Dana and Ashley, to engage them. Nate, good 'soldier' that he is, kept his eyes on his area of responsibility, watching our backs.

I triggered off three rounds as fast as I could lever them into the chamber of my rifle. I scored two good headshots, and my third shot clipped an adult male zombie in the shoulder. I could hear Ashley's handgun clapping off rounds at a steady rate, and I knew that she was having minimal effect. The engagement distance was past twenty-five yards, and I knew she was firing body shots. None of them would stop the zombies, but the impact of the bullets into the zombie bodies would slow them down some... maybe. Either way I was proud that she was in the fight and not cowering behind me just waiting to die or be zombiefied. None of my family would go down without a strong fight and, given the current reality, that was the best I could hope for.

Johnny was aiming his shots carefully, but I watched as he fired twice and both times the bullets failed to puncture the cranial vault of the zombies. In other words, the bullets weren't punching through the bone. They were probably too light. I heard Dana's shotgun boom and saw puffs of dust and gray yuck dance off the zombie farthest to the left, but the shotgun round she fired must have been buckshot because the holes made were all pretty small (as compared to a slug).

Recognizing that I needed to take out the three remaining zombies with headshots, I took careful aim and fired my next shot, satisfied to see another zombie head explode into bits of gray tissue, straggly hair and white mucus. At the same time I did that I heard Nate yell behind me and just to my left. "Contact right!" He fired his weapon immediately.

As I levered up my next round and took aim, I realized that Nate was firing his rounds at a fair pace. Out of the corner of my eye I also saw Dana turn and heard her shotgun boom again... and again... and again. That fast she had worked the action and fired. Either she had fallen into an unnecessary panic or those zombies behind us were damned close.

I fired and hit the fourth zombie in the head and levered up my next round. Aiming carefully, I heard Ashley's handgun join the fight going on behind me (for all intents and purposes). I triggered off my shot and was satisfied to see the last zombie fall. "Hold front, Johnny!" I said before I turned, my hand reaching for more rounds to jam into the tubular magazine of my rifle. What I saw as I turned around scared me – badly.

I forced my hands to keep functioning, reloading my rifle as my eyes took in the scene. I don't know where they'd all come from but I saw better than two dozen zombies shuffling toward us and another five or six laying on the ground, their heads leaking or with chunks missing.

As I aimed and fired my next round it dawned, on me that we needed to keep moving rather than standing still and fighting a static position engagement. "Moving!" I shouted above the shots. I felt little Ashley's hand grab my belt as I began to shuffle-step to my left, my eyes swinging back and forth between the direction we were traveling in and the direction the zombies were coming from. Dana and Nate continued to fire as we moved, and I realized that we had limited eyeballs checking our perimeter.

Still moving and still shooting, I did my best to adjust and, God love 'em, my family adjusted with me. "Johnny!" I called out. "Take rear guard from your position."

"Got it!" he yelled back.

"Ashley!" I yelled. "Take left guard but stay holding onto me if you can."

"Okay, dad!" she yelled back. I could barely hear her tiny voice over the din of the gunfire and the ringing in my ears.

Our pace of travel was slow, and even that reduced the accuracy with which we were shooting the zombies. I guessed that we were down to less than twenty coming after us, but one was too many and we weren't knocking them down fast enough. Looking for a silver lining, I was silently thankful that zombies couldn't run, except in the movies.

One of the biggest challenges we faced was that my rifle only held seven rounds in the magazine. I had to make every shot count because reloading took too long (especially since we still had well over a dozen zombies stalking after us). Dana's shotgun was the same way: seven rounds in the magazine. We both could work the guns to shoot seven rounds in well under five seconds – even shooting accurately. But reloading seven rounds took almost twice as long, and we were constantly distracted by two things:

1) The zombies that were not slowing down as they kept coming after us, and

2) Our footing. Even as we were shooting on the move, we were double checking that we wouldn't trip or turn an ankle. In this type of situation, a sprained ankle could well mean death.

"Reloading!" I heard Dana yell as she racked open the action of her shotgun. Even as she yelled it I fired my last shot and opened the action on an empty magazine time. I knew that I couldn't reload right then because we simply couldn't have two guns out of the fight leaving Nate as the only family/team member shooting, but my rifle was empty. Without pause, holding the rifle in my left hand, I drew my handgun, brought it up into my line of sight, and began engaging zombies with it. Although I hated that the zombies seemed to be steadily getting closer, I was also appreciative of the fact that they were close enough for my .45 caliber handgun to be effective.

I didn't even notice what the zombies looked like that we were shooting. Adult, child, adolescent, male, female... it didn't matter. If it was gray and shambling toward us with its arms up and its eyes a mix of milky white and chalk gray, we were delivering head shots. Nothing NOT zombie would be in the middle of them, so we were free to shoot without worrying about "collateral damage" provided we didn't shoot each other.

I heard Dana's shotgun boom again and knew she was back in the fight. I had to reload fast. "Reloading!" I shouted as I holstered my handgun. At almost the same moment Nate yelled, "Reloading!" and I knew we had put ourselves in a bad spot. He and I both hesitated and made it that much worse.

"Do it!" I yelled at him even as I dropped my rifle and drew my handgun again. I shot with my right hand as I reached for a fresh magazine with my left hand. I only had a couple shots left in my pistol before the slide locked back and I had to reload it. Thankfully, reloading a pistol is a half-second operation, and Nate could reload his rifle in about two seconds or less.

I saw him bring his rifle back up and muzzle flash flame out the end of the barrel just after I had reloaded my handgun. I started to holster my handgun so I could pick up my rifle, and it was only then that I realized we had never stopped moving. My rifle was ten feet behind us and getting farther away with every shuffle-step we took. At that point, it might as well have been on the moon. It was empty and out of reach. In that instant of realization, my handgun became my primary weapon.

Before we had knocked down all the zombies, Dana had reloaded again, as had I. I had six loaded magazines for my pistol plus whatever was still in it and one empty magazine. I had a couple boxes of ammo for it in my pack, but I'd have to stop to get that out and stuff rounds into the empty magazines before it would be usable.

We were still moving and, after making sure none of the zombies behind us were mobile, we all resumed our travel responsibilities based on where we were in our diamond: me on point, Dana on rear guard, Nate on the right, Johnny on the left and Ashley once again protected in the middle. As we prepared to move, I heard her perform a reload and was silently thankful for the time we'd invested training at home.

"Halt!" I called, confident of our security for the moment. Yes, I knew there were zombies in the area; yes, we had just shot more than two dozen of them, and there was no way to know how many more those shots would attract. No, I didn't have my rifle, and, as I looked, it was less than fifty yards away, laying on the ground several yards from the nearest zombie corpse. I wanted my rifle. We needed the longer range capacity and the punch of the heavier bullets. Not that we didn't have the range with Johnny and Nate's rifles, but their rifles fired lighter rounds, and the more firepower we had, the better off we'd be. It was another one of those unwritten rules: You can never have too much firepower.

I knew I was going back for my rifle. I was of two minds about how to do it best. It wasn't that far, but I had to step out of what I considered our protective circle to do it. Part of me wanted to get a handful of ammo for the rifle in my hand so I could pick it up and immediately start stuffing them in the magazine. Part of me knew better, demanding that I keep my handgun in hand and ready whether I was leaving the circle of safety or not. Either way, I knew was going back. I had to let my family know.

"Hold this position," I said firmly. "I'm going for my rifle. If I get attacked or go down, DO NOT come and get me. Continue on with the previous plan of travel." A chorus of, "Got it," and "Roger that," came back to me. "Ashley," I said to insure I had her attention.

"Yeah, dad?"

"Cover my spot 'til I get back."

"Yes, sir," she said. As I moved out of my position on point, she stepped in to fill it, her handgun looking in the same direction as her eyes, and those actively seeking any threat that might present itself.

I glanced at my wife as I stepped past her, and I could see from the look on her face that she didn't like what I was doing. Movement was security. Standing still made everyone potentially vulnerable. She didn't like that eight-year-old Ashley was now fully responsible for a position, and she didn't like the idea of leaving me if anything ugly happened. She understood all of it but didn't like it. Her unhappiness was one of the reasons I only held the glance for the briefest of moments. The other reason was that I wanted to scan as much of the area around me before I moved into it as I could.

The potential threat areas were the barn I was now moving back toward and the house slightly farther away off to my right. There was nothing but open space around both structures, and I felt pretty confident that we had killed every zombie that had been hiding in the barn. Moving into a sprint, I considered that last thought: I had no way of knowing if we'd killed every zombie in the barn. We had killed every zombie that came out of the barn after us.

I was painfully aware of every second that passed. It only took me a few to get to my rifle, grab it with my left hand, keeping my .45 ready in my right fist, and then turn to run back toward my family. There was still no threat in sight anywhere I could see, and I experienced a moment of pride as I looked at my family. Their postures were all confident. Everyone was "in the game:" their eyes were searching for any threat, and their guns were all up just under their line of sight.

I hot-footed it back to that protective circle and stopped in the middle. Before relieving Ashley of her responsibility at point, I had to load my rifle. Holstering my handgun, I quickly fed seven jacketed soft-nose rounds into the rifle, levering the first one up into the chamber and then feeding another round into the magazine.

As I stepped up next to Ashley, I eased the hammer on my rifle down to the half-cock notch and said, "I'm on point."

"Roger that," said my little girl in a voice so serious I'd have smiled if I hadn't been, in that moment, so terribly aware of the fact her life was in danger. Maybe the danger wasn't immediate, but it was in danger just the same; all of our lives were.

"Moving," I said, receiving the same chorus of acknowledgements I had earlier. I felt better as we continued to move across the farm's fields. Ahead of us was the edge of the forest and, off to our left in the distance, a roadway. I had to decide whether to go through the woods, which was dangerous because of the limited fields of view, or head for the roadway, which was dangerous because zombies tended to travel the easiest path, and roads presented pretty easy traveling for them. I didn't have to voice a decision to my family. They'd move with me in whatever direction I wanted to travel. Unless I wanted to turn left, right or go back, we'd move along as the coordinated gun team we had become through training.

I decided to travel the shortest distance to our destination, meaning we were heading through the woods. I did some mental math and guessed we'd only be in the woods for a couple of hundred yards at most before we'd reach either another farm or the park. I knew we could probably make better time on the roads, but that assumption was predicated on not running into any zombies or healthy human predators – and there were still plenty of those around.

None of us said a word as we moved until we got closer to the trees. "Spread," I commanded and received confirmation that everyone heard me. "Ashley, close up closer to me," I added. The change in our formation meant a little extra distance between the four corners of our diamond, but Ashley was right up behind me, practically walking in my boot prints.

WEAPONS

GUNS

Setting aside the politics of the gun control versus 2nd Amendment debate and dismissing the fiction that every country in the world controls small arms except America, recognize that personally owned firearms and adequate preparation are the two main reasons that zombies haven't overrun the entire planet. Make no mistake, zombies are higher on the food chain than humans simply because they carry the virus. They are capable of transferring that virus to every other land mammal alive thereby increasing their hunting efficiency in an incalculable fashion.

Preparing to defend against the zombies and protecting yourself from infection are paramount concerns. Defending against zombies is best done at a distance, and only guns do sufficient damage at the distances that make a difference. So, if you want to debate the pros or cons of gun control, find another time and place to do it. The reality is this: if you want to survive zombie outbreak you will purchase, train with, and carry appropriate firearms. Let's look at some of the various types of firearms available to discuss the strengths or weaknesses of each type.

LEVER ACTION RIFLES

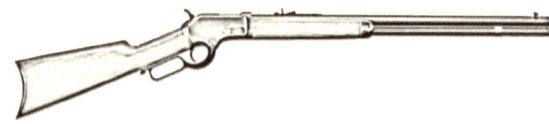

Although many of us think of western movies and cowboys when we see these, the truth is that they are excellent hunting weapons, and more than one person has considered them as effective rifles for police use – even in contemporary times. You can get them chambered either for rifle calibers (.308, .30-.30, .444 Marlin and more) OR you can get them chambered for handgun calibers (.357 Magnum, .44 Magnum, etc.). No matter your caliber choice, the large majority of lever action rifles provide sufficient head ventilating capability to make them good zombie stopping weapons.

If you want to simplify your ammunition needs, matching your rifle to your handgun can make sense. In this case, if your primary sidearm (handgun) is going to be a revolver or semi-auto chambered in .357 Magnum or .44 Magnum (or other caliber available in a lever action rifle), then it makes sense to have a rifle in that caliber. The potential accuracy of a lever action rifle is excellent, and, even with the magnum handgun ammunition mentioned, you can reach out to 300 or 400 yards effectively. With rifle caliber lever actions, you're usually limited to five to seven rounds of ammo capacity in the tubular under barrel magazine, but with handgun calibers, you can sometimes get ten or more rounds in the magazine depending on the caliber and the barrel length. Additionally, in a zombie outbreak situation, law enforcement officers might perceive these lever-action weapons as less "aggressive" than some other styles of rifle.

SHOTGUNS

The potential versatility of shotguns, thanks to the ammunition availability, makes them highly valuable in any survival situation; and make no mistake, a zombie outbreak IS a survival situation. You can get shotguns in several configurations today: side-by-side or over-under double barrel shotguns, pump action shotguns or semi-automatic shotguns. Unless you have the expertise to operate and maintain the semi-auto weapon, it's recommended that you use a pump action shotgun. The double-barrel weapons are certainly devastating in the damage they can do, but you only get two shots and then you have to manually reload two more rounds... Simplicity is one of the pump shotgun's greatest strengths. They are relatively easy to understand in function, field strip, clean and reassemble. Pump action shotguns are easy to load, easy to operate and easy to unload.

Shotguns are not small though, and there is no hiding one; however, they are easily recognized by anyone who has ever watched television or movies, and they are generally thought to be devastating weapons. The sound of the action working is almost universally recognized and will make bad guys think twice about attacking (there is no evidence that zombies will know or recognize this sound; however, during a zombie outbreak, the zombies aren't the only predators you have to worry about, and human bad guys will think twice when they hear the action work.)

Ammunition versatility (as mentioned) is also a strength of the shotgun. With ammo types ranging from slugs (single projectile) to twelve-shot (LOTS of small pellets), changing ammo can alter the purpose of the shotgun. For example, if you're using it as a defense weapon, 00 buck (nine .32 caliber pellets in a 2.75″ shell) might be best, but if you're hunting squab for food, then 8-shot (or smaller) would be better. For zombie outbreak situations, we recommend a shotgun without a choke, but different folks like different things. Anything that limits your weapon use should be avoided for zombie outbreak survival planning and preparation. There is such a plethora of ammunition designs for the twelve gauge that you may experience a challenge figuring out how to prioritize what you need and how to place it. Prioritize it thus: your first choice in ammo should be what will vaporize a zombie's head inside an engagement distance of 25 yards. Such will also be effective, if necessary, against human predators as well.

Capacity is one challenge of the shotgun. With a standard tubular magazine holding five rounds or less, you either want to be real good at reloading or you have to plan accordingly. Shotguns set up for hunting (in most places) have a three-shot maximum capacity. *Defense* shotguns can be expanded though: as an example, a police officer friend of mine has a Remington 870 with a 7-shot tubular magazine, a 5-shot "side saddle" shell holder (on the side of the receiver) and a 6-shot shell holder on the stock for a total of 18 rounds available in or on the weapon itself. Using a MOLLE thigh platform and two 18-round shotgun ammo holders, you can have 36 rounds more in a single location that is easily carried.

A sling is almost mandatory for any large weapon (which the shotgun is, and more ammo can be put on the sling in bandoleer fashion) because otherwise you're permanently committing one hand to carrying the weapon. That's better than not having it at all, but the ability to sling it and have both hands available to fight zombies, climb, blockade doors, etc., is preferred. The after-market shotgun accessory business is booming, and you can "dress" your shotgun however you see necessary. If you add anything to or modify your shotgun, make sure you practice with the new configuration. If you add a light, remember that you need replacement bulbs and batteries – otherwise all you've done is add weight to the front end of the weapon

SEMI-AUTOMATIC RIFLES

The "black rifle," which was a nickname coined for the M16 but has come to include virtually all M16/AR-style rifles, is an excellent weapon. Many people see it strictly as a combat

weapon, although I do know some folks who think it makes a good hunting rifle. Either way, during a zombie crisis, you will either be using it for combat (against zombies), combat (against human predators), or hunting (for food if you're traveling).

Understand up front that if this is your zombie outbreak survival weapon of choice any government representative you encounter is going to think you've got the rifle for violent purposes instead of hunting or zombie survival. Why? It is an unfortunate side effect of media impact on our perceptions. After all, when was the last time you saw a television show or movie where someone used an AR-style rifle for hunting? They're always portrayed as combat weapons.

That said, plenty of semi-automatic rifles are available that don't resemble the M16/AR-style weapons in any way beyond having a shared caliber. Such weapons are typically viewed as hunting weapons, although they can easily and efficiently serve as zombie killing weapons as well.

During a zombie outbreak, to increase your chance of finding the ammo you need for your particular weapon, choose a common caliber. Now, I know some folks who argue the other way. Their outlook is that, in a crisis, LOTS of people are going to be looking for .308 and .223, and therefore those ammo supplies will run out fast, making it more desirable to have an uncommon caliber weapon.

Most of the folks who have set up a "zombie outbreak survival kit" and have included a "black rifle" have at least five to seven magazines loaded and ready to go. That's 150 to 210 rounds of ammo. It might be a little while before they have to find more.

ZOMBIE STOPPER SIGHTING SYSTEM

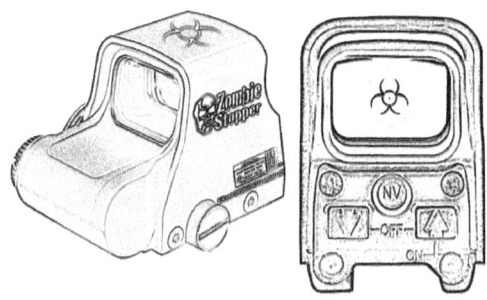

In a conflict situation where you need to engage your target as accurately as possible but as quickly as possible, you need a sighting system that lets you see "the whole picture" while also aiming your weapon. Prior to the public release of information about zombie outbreaks, one company – EOTech – manufactured a "zombie stopper" holographic optic. While they were attempting to leverage the existing zombie craze to increase sales, they actually produced not only an excellent sighting system but also a constant reminder of the true zombie threat: the biohazard that exists within every cell of a zombie's body.

Using the internationally recognized biohazard symbol as the reticle, EOTech unintentionally created a visual reminder of the threat. It's viewed every time a weapon using this sight is aimed, reminding the shooter exactly why they must be accurate in shot placement while offering them an ideal tool to be accurate with shot placement.

HANDGUNS

Springfield Armory
Government Model
1911 .45ACP

The Government Model 1911 .45ACP semi-automatic handgun was invented in 1904 by James Browning. It was entered into the U.S. Army trials as they sought a new handgun to replace the .38 Special revolver. With a few modifications it was adopted by the U.S. Army in 1911, hence the name: Government Model 1911. It served as the sidearm of choice for the U.S. Army and other military branches until 1985 when it was replaced by a 9mm handgun, bringing the U.S. military into compliance with NATO caliber weapons.

In March of 2011, just prior to the publicly recognized announcement of the ongoing zombie outbreaks, it celebrated 100 years of service. It still remained, at that point, one of the most popular personal sidearms. Depending on the manufacturer and model, it would hold anywhere from seven to fifteen rounds of .45ACP ammo, which – at reasonable handgun engagement distances – was an efficient zombie stopper. With an entry hole that was almost one-half inch in diameter and an exit wound that was often four to five times that, the .45ACP bullet did sufficient brain tissue damage to shut down zombies decisively.

Justin Rustovic's 1911 of choice was manufactured by Springfield Armory. This standard-sized steel framed pistol, depending on the magazines used, held eight or nine rounds of ammunition, although Justin had several ten-round magazines as well. When inserted, they stuck out of the bottom of the grip about two inches. While it may have looked a tad off-balance, no one argued about having eleven rounds of .45ACP ammo in the gun. Once zombie outbreaks had been accepted as reality, the general thought was, "there's no such thing as too much ammo."

Because of the popularity of the Government Model 1911 weapon and the ongoing use of it both in the civilian market and in the military special operations community, ammunition for it remains readily available. Virtually every major handgun manufacturer makes one or more models chambered for the .45ACP, and the accessories market for Government Model 1911 style pistols is vast, allowing for users to select holsters, sights, etc., with ease.

Both the Glock Model 17 (above) and the Glock Model 19 (below) are chambered for the 9mm Parabellum (9x19 as you can see stamped on the side of each weapon) cartridge.

Being the NATO standard handgun caliber, ammo for both is abundant.

The Glock Model 17 was the first handgun produced by that weapons manufacturer. Although this model does hold seventeen rounds of ammo in a standard magazine, that was not why it was designated "Model 17." It was, in fact, Dr. Glock's seventeenth patent, so he named it the Model 17. It was specifically developed to be entered into the U.S. Army's handgun selection competition in the early 1980s as they sought to replace the Government Model 1911 with a weapon in the standard NATO handgun caliber. Although Glock did not win that competition, it did all but take over the law enforcement market in the United States and became popular with many military organizations around the world. With a polymer frame and three safeties that disengaged and re-engaged automatically when the trigger is pulled, the Glock Model 17 remains a popular handgun in both the civilian and law enforcement markets.

Due to her hand size and the manageability of recoil, Dana Rustovic prefers the Glock Model 17 over handguns in larger calibers and over all revolvers (which have no recoil absorbing system). With nineteen rounds of 9mm ammo per magazine (she uses extended floorplates on her magazines that add two rounds per) and having seven magazines available, Dana carries over 150 rounds of ammo JUST for her handgun.

Some readers will note the skip from Model 17 9mm to Model 19 9mm. The Glock Model 18 – not shown here, nor used by the Rustovic family – is a select fire pistol. Using 30+ round magazines, it has a switch that will put the pistol in safe, or single shot, or triple shot mode. Yes, you can pull the trigger once and get three rounds out of the weapon. Do not mistake either the Model 17 or the Model 19 for a select fire weapon. They are both semi-automatic only (one trigger pull = one shot fired).

Nate Rustovic chose the Glock Model 19 as his sidearm. Each standard magazine holds fifteen rounds of 9mm ammunition, and he has seven magazines. He made the same modification to his magazines that Dana did to hers, giving each of his magazines a seventeen-round capacity. So, with seven magazines, he carries over 110 rounds of 9mm ammo, 18 of them in the gun. The barrel of the Model 19 is one-half inch shorter than that of the Model 17, but no appreciable difference in accuracy is noticed.

Nate's Model 19 has the additional strength of being able to use the magazines out of Dana's gun, although she can't do the same with his. The Model 17 magazines will fit and lock into the Model 19's magazine well, but the Model 19 magazines are not long enough to lock into the Model 17's magazine well.

Sig Sauer P226 9mm

Johnny's handgun of choice is the Sig Sauer P226 chambered for the 9mm NATO round. He has three fifteen-round magazines for it. Chambering the first round and then topping off the magazine in the weapon gives me sixteen rounds in the gun with thirty more rounds for reload. The Sig P226 gained quite a following in the U.S. Navy Special Warfare community and was adopted by a number of police departments in the late 1980s.

It is unique among most 9mm semi-automatic pistols selected by law enforcement agencies in that it doesn't have a manual safety. It is a double-action/single-action weapon meaning that it is carried with a round chambered and the hammer down. After chambering the first round, the user pulls down the decocking lever, dropping the hammer safely to a rest position.

The first trigger pull thereafter is "double-action" meaning that it performs two actions: it cocks the hammer and then releases the hammer to strike the firing pin, discharging the weapon. After the first shot is fired, the slide cycles to the rear, extracting and ejecting the spent case from the chamber and cocking the hammer before moving forward again under spring pressure, loading the next cartridge into the firing chamber along the way. The second shot, and each one thereafter until the weapon is manually decocked, is fired "single action" meaning that pulling the trigger performs only a single function – that of dropping the hammer to fire the round.

FN Herstal 5.7 mm pistol

Ashley, at the grand old age of eight, doesn't have hands one would think big enough or strong enough to manage a full-size handgun; however, the FN Herstal FiveSeven, chambered for their proprietary 5.7mm round, holds 20 rounds of ammo per magazine and has the recoil of a light .22. Although the grip is a bit long for Ashley's hands, so she has to use two to hold it, the recoil is light enough that she can put rounds accurately on target and get pretty quick follow-up shots. The 5.7mm round isn't a very large bullet (5.56mm = .223, so the 5.7mm isn't much bigger in diameter than a regular .22) but it exits the weapon at a pretty high velocity. Since the energy delivered to the target is dependent on the size of the bullet combined with its velocity, this high-velocity comparatively-small-mass bullet still delivers sufficient energy to scramble a zombie brain.

The larger challenge is that Ashley simply doesn't have the hand strength to pull the slide back to chamber the first round if it's being dry loaded; that being loaded from an empty condition. So, one of her older brothers or one of her parents has to originally load it for her. If she shoots it until the magazine is empty and the slide locks back, she can reload it and pull down the slide-stop to release the slide, thereby loading the weapon.

SWORDS

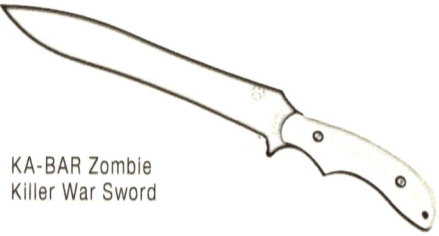

KA-BAR Zombie
Killer War Sword

Although many people would argue whether the KA-BAR ZK War Sword is actually a sword, research has revealed no minimum required blade length for the term. Historically speaking, the use of the tool more determined whether it was deemed a knife or a sword. The Roman Gladius, a "short sword," wasn't much longer than many of today's "survival knives." The difference is that the sword is used to chop, hack and thrust as a weapon of aggression. A knife is typically used as a utility tool to cut, chop or hack inanimate objects. Thus defined, the KA-BAR ZK War Sword is appropriately named.

The ZK War Sword, with its almost ten-inch long blade and over five inches of handle, is suitable for splitting open a zombie skull or simply decapitating the creature. If the zombie is reaching for you, the ZK War Sword is sharp enough, out of the box, to remove that reaching limb.

Where swords and other hacking/chopping tools are concerned, it is imperative to remember two things:

First, it's all about reach and destruction. You don't want the zombie to get close enough to touch you, so the length of the blade plus the handle plus your arm has to be longer than the zombie's reach AND still do the necessary damage.

Second, NEVER NEVER NEVER NEVER use your fighting blades for other camp or survival chores. There is simply no way to guarantee that you've removed all trace of zombie cellular material from the blade once you've used it as a weapon against them. Even a single cell carries the zombie virus, so you don't want to risk contaminating your other utility items or food preparation tools.

Along this vein, longer swords are obviously better, but they have the downside of being less maneuverable and are (usually) heavier. A happy compromise on a sword blade length between fifteen and twenty-five inches is recommended.

HATCHETS/AXES/TOMAHAWKS

Many a "horror" movie has been made with scenes wherein the good guy hacks the bad guy in the head with an axe, hatchet or tomahawk. In fact, many a horror movie has been made where it's worked the other way around as well. The bottom line? Wedge shaped blades, such as those found on these tools, do awesome amounts of damage to cranial structure if the strength of the person swinging the tool is sufficient.

In the case of the Rustovic family, both Justin and his son, Johnny, have tomahawks mounted on their packs. Although they don't carry the 'hawks with the intended purpose of weaponry, both have practiced striking head-shaped objects so that they'd be skilled with these weapons if necessary.

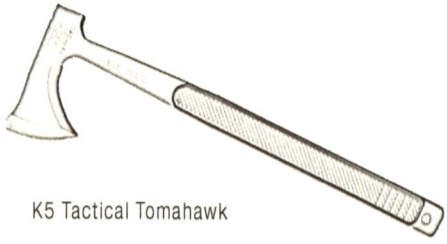

K5 Tactical Tomahawk

The difference between Justin and Johnny's 'hawks is that Johnny's is a model that was designed primarily for camping/ survival use while Justin's was designed for survival/breaching use. Both of them have sharp, properly shaped blade heads. Both of them have handles with a pry-bar end designed in. Both are manufactured from a single piece of hammer-forged steel. The difference is the backside of the blade end. Johnny's 'hawk has a backside that can be used for hammering.

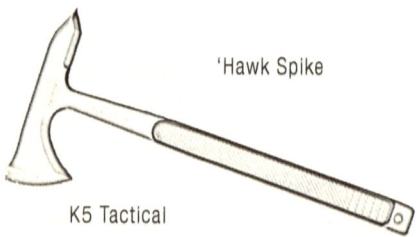

'Hawk Spike

K5 Tactical

Justin's has a backside that is, as the name "Hawk Spike" indicates, spiked. The spike was designed in expressly for the purpose of fighting with this tomahawk OR using it to break into or "breach" structures. As necessary, the spike would certainly breach a zombie's cranial structure without much effort on Justin's part.

KNIVES

Knives are a necessary utility tool in any survival or camping scenario. In fact, knives are necessary utility tools even at home in your kitchen in the most peaceful of times. The difference is the circumstance you find yourself using that knife in and what abuse or environment conditions the knife might need to survive.

In the case of Justin and his family, an assortment of knives are carried and available, but the Famine Tanto, part of that Zombie Killer line from KA-BAR, is favored by Justin and his wife, Dana. With (about) a 7.5" blade, the Famine Tanto isn't small, but it's not long enough for its primary purpose to be hacking or chopping. It cuts pretty well, and the Tanto style blade is specifically designed for thrusting strength.

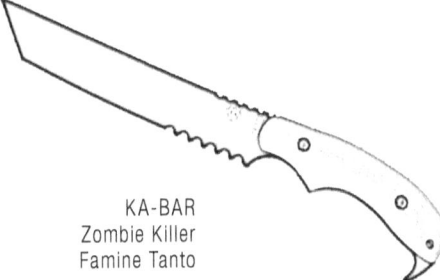

KA-BAR
Zombie Killer
Famine Tanto

Other knives that the family members carry range in size from blades three inches long to seven inches long, all with differing blade types and carry methods. The one consideration they all have is sterilization of utility: no family member uses a knife as a weapon during a zombie attack. Once they do, that knife is either dedicated as a zombie fighting weapon or it's discarded. Every family member has a fixed blade utility knife as well as a folding lockblade knife as a redundant back up. The necessity of a utility knife cannot be excused or overlooked in a survival/ zombie combat situation.

FIRE

As Justin and his family learned, a hot fire is the only good way to destroy a zombie body. That said, human flesh, animated or otherwise, is not efficient fire fuel. To burn a zombie's body you need an external fuel source to accelerate the burning process and help the rotted flesh reach a temperature where it will burn efficiently and completely.

Gasoline and magnesium both make good accelerators if you're doing a "zombie burn." If, however, you intend to use fire as a weapon against zombies, then you might want to rethink. Fire, when used as a weapon, has to be hot enough to do fast damage to whatever muscle structure they have left; otherwise it will do nothing to slow them down. Remember, zombies don't feel pain.

Also, you can't plan to use fire to blind them as they also hunt by sound and smell. There is even one theory that they can hunt based on the electro-magnetic pulses of a living human heart, so burning their face/eyes/nose won't do you much good.

If you intend to use fire as a weapon against zombies, then there are a couple of considerations. First, you have to get close enough to use it but not so close that it burns you too. Second, you have to project it somehow: a flame thrower or improvised fire bombs can work if you have the means and the materials to build them. Third, you have to project enough fire to do that fast damage in enough quantity to hinder their progress. Fourth, you have to go back and finish the job. It is irresponsible to light a zombie on fire and then leave them as you make your escape. If you light them on fire, you are duty-bound, in the contemporary world of zombie outbreaks, to stay within visual distance and, once they're incapable of further movement, go back to finish incinerating them.

EXPLOSIVES

Explosives are a bozo no-no when it comes to fighting zombies. While many people are eager to find a stash of grenades, or build their own, to blow up zombies, sure in the knowledge that it will stop the zombies from pursuit, those same people forget that every single cell in a zombie's body contains the Solanum (or whatever it is) virus. Explosively scattering microscopic bits of zombie flesh is a bad idea.

That said, there are times when explosives can be used to contain or bury zombies. For example, if you have managed to run through a structure as you are pursued by zombies AND you can manage to trap them in that structure, then blowing it down around them, hopefully burning them under the rubble, is a good thing.

IMPACT WEAPONS

As we learned early on, impact weapons can be effective but only if they are used to cause sufficient damage to the cranial structure to either also damage the brain OR to deconstruct the bone structure that holds the brain in place. What that means is that any impact tool, such as a nightstick or baseball bat, that might be easily used to knock out a human being (make them unconscious), will have no effect on a zombie. To stop a zombie, that impact weapon has to be used in such a manner and with such force that the skull is actually broken open and damage done to the brain.

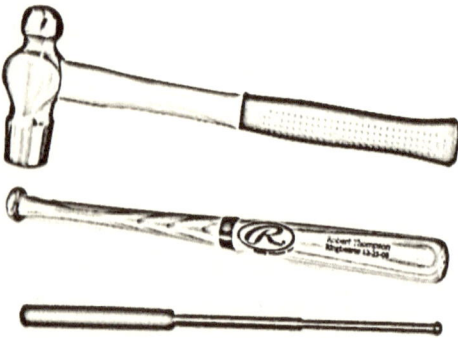

The largest concern when using any type of impact weapon is zombie goo splatter. Remembering that virtually every cell of a zombie's body is infected and, therefore, infectious, it's imperative that you protect yourself from the splatter if you are forced into a situation where you're fighting a zombie using an impact weapon. Your face must be protected to include your eyes (goggles are your friend) and your mouth (surgical masks, painter's masks, etc., work well). If you get splatter onto your skin, wash it as soon as is practical with water as hot as you can stand it and antibacterial soap. Many "scholars" debate the value of using antibacterials to fight something viral, but, as was noted earlier on, zombies also carry other infections and diseases. Take all appropriate precautions and do anything safe that you think might help in minimizing your chance of exposure and/or infection.

IMPROVISED WEAPONS

An "improvised weapon" is anything not specifically designed for use as a weapon but that you employ as a weapon dependent on the circumstances. If you use your vehicle to run down zombies, you're using it as an improvised weapon. If you pick up a wooden chair and hit a zombie with it, you're using it as an improvised weapon.

There are two important things to remember about improvised weapons:

First, the limit of what you can use as one and how you can cause damage to zombies with it is only your imagination.

Second, because of the nature of improvisation, sometimes you get results that are both unpredictable and uncontainable; therefore, you must have at least a reasonable idea of the expected results before deploying your improvised weaponry of any kind.

Keeping those two considerations in mind, expand your consciousness (and your education) and improvise any weapon that will help you survive a zombie outbreak and destroy zombies in the process. Do some Internet research and learn what combinations of what cleaners under your kitchen sink can be combined to create explosives. Learn what food stuffs you have in your pantry (yes, there are some) that can be combined with other household items to create caustic and/or explosive packages.

18

I LEARNED THE VALUE OF "ANTIQUE" WEAPONRY

As dictated by Justin Rustovic and notated by Frank Borelli.

The trees weren't as deep as I thought, and we were out of them, I'd guess, in less than fifteen minutes. It seemed a long fifteen minutes as we traveled cautiously, with our senses wide open and seeking out any sign or sound that would indicate a zombie presence. While I had often enjoyed hikes through the woods as a child, and even in my young adult years, it had become an intimidating experience. All those cute little critters I used to enjoy seeing during my hikes – animals like rabbits, squirrels, chipmunks, and such – were now potential carriers of death. The good news was that, for the most part, unless they were rabid, they fled upon our approach. The bad news was that we had no way of guaranteeing we wouldn't come across a rabid animal, and rabies was far from being the biggest threat in this new reality.

On the other side of the trees were more fields, a farm house several hundred yards farther on, and several outbuildings I assumed held miscellaneous items for farm tending. Again,

I tried to plan our route of travel so that we didn't get too close to any of the buildings, allowing for the greatest amount of reactionary time if an attack came. There was another line of trees in the distance but I guessed it to be at least a mile away and most of that mile was plowed fields or grass.

We had moved about fifty or sixty yards out of the tree line when I heard the first bark. It echoed off the buildings in front of me and the trees behind me so I couldn't accurately identify which direction it had come from. Several more followed immediately after the first bark, but they all echoed to the point of being overwhelming and not identifiable in location of origin. We didn't stop moving, but I knew all of us were looking around more aggressively; our heads were moving like they were on a permanent swivel.

The first dog came out of the nearest outbuilding at a full run headed straight for us. It was small enough not to be able to transform into a zombie, but that really didn't matter. It was coming at us, fast, in an aggressive fashion, and we knew that ANY mammal could be a carrier of the zombie virus. Being bitten, or even scratched, could mean infection, death and transformation. None of us was going to let that happen. Still, hitting a target like a medium-sized, fast-moving dog isn't so easy. My mind spun through the options, and I said one word. "Dana."

My wife knew my intent and swung her shotgun around, aimed, fired and pumped the action, ready to fire a second shot if it was necessary. It wasn't. The buckshot didn't spread far, and several of the pellets hit the dog, the energy of the shot catching it in the face and chest. If it wasn't such a serious situation, I'd have laughed as the dog's back end didn't realize the front end had stopped and it tumbled ass over teakettle until it finally rolled to a stop and lay twitching.

The noise of the barking didn't stop though. It grew like the sound of approaching motorcycles or a herd of horses, soon loud enough that it drowned out even the ringing in my ears caused by the boom of Dana's shotgun. Then we saw them…

From out of and around the same building the first dog had come from, dozens more seemed to just flow. It looked as if the building was vomiting dogs as they came out of it at a full run; every one of them looking mean; every one of them barking as it came; every one of them too small to be zombiefied but still a threat. I had never seen a pack of dogs as big as this, but I did a quick scan of the ones I could see, and none of them looked big enough to have turned. Still, even without the threat of a zombie infection, no one likes to get bitten. WITH the threat of zombie infection, even kittens can make grown adults feel fear.

They were approaching from our front and right, so Dana, Johnny, Ashley and I engaged them. Nate held our left, and I knew he'd do his best to watch the rear as well. We needed Dana's shotgun and its spread shot capability in this fight. For half a moment I felt deep sorrow at the thought of Ashley and the fear she must be experiencing, but I didn't have time to express that sorrow, and there was no way to process it, so I set it aside and focused on the fight. The best we could do was stay alive and uninfected so we could comfort her after the fact.

Johnny fired faster than either Dana or I, with Ashley firing her handgun nearly as fast as he was firing his rifle. I couldn't tell if she was scoring hits, and if she was if they were slowing or stopping any of the hounds. I couldn't take the time to worry about it. We were in a race. If even one dog got to us to inflict injury, we'd lost the race. If we knocked them all down before a single one could get to us, we'd won – and we'd get to live, not transformed, to fight another day.

At first I felt like the dogs were winning this life or death race. Even through the din of our gunfire I was all too aware that not enough dogs were falling. Dana's shotgun stopped three, sometimes four at a time. Johnny's rifle kept spitting lead, and each of his shots seemed to coincide with a dog stumbling or falling. I fired as fast as I could lever rounds up, and each of my shots, thanks to the heavy, fast-moving loads, would go through the first dog hit and hit at least one more. Depending on the size of the first two, I might get lucky and have the round punch through to stop another one.

Dogs can run fast, and the tide of canine teeth had to be turned faster. Within just a second or two it seemed like they'd closed half the distance on us, but it also looked like we'd stopped half or more of them. As dogs fell and the pack thinned out, they also spread out, creating more space between them and forcing us to pick our shots more carefully.

I estimated that they'd be on us in another three or four seconds maximum, and I had that thought at the same moment I fired the eighth round out of my rifle. Dropping the gun for the second time that day (two times too many in my opinion), I drew my handgun and started shooting. The dogs were close enough, and closing fast, that it was pretty easy to make my shots count.

And then there were only four or five dogs still coming. The rest were laying in a mass of bloody fur and meat scattered across the ground between us and the building they'd come from. Dana's shotgun boomed again, and I saw two of the dogs spin before falling. Johnny's rifle barked and another dog fell. Ashley fired a shot and then yelled, "I'm out!" as her slide locked back. There was an edge of panic in her voice and she hadn't scored a hit. The dogs were almost on us. I fired a shot and put one of the dogs down, and my slide locked back as well. One dog was left, and it was close enough that I could see the red around the yellow iris of its eyes and the saliva spray from it jowls with every bark. A small part of my brain registered the fact that even the saliva was potentially deadly.

Before I could think, the dog was in the air, having launched itself at Johnny. I tried to reload and pull my knife both at the same time. When you try to do two things that require a total of three hands, you end up dropping something. In this case, I dropped my handgun. Johnny's rifle stock impacted the dog's ribcage as he butt-stroked it with all his strength. The dog spun toward me in midair, still snarling and snapping, flailing its claws and trying to bite anything it could.

With my knife now drawn, I caught the dog by the neck and, at the same moment, sank my blade into it, pushing the steel in behind its shoulder, doing my best to force the tip all the way through and out the other side. I was thinking of the ideal gunshot – not a head shot – to stop an animal: in behind the shoulder, traverse the heart and lungs, and out the other shoulder. I was trying to push my knife through the same path to most quickly stop this thing from trying to bite or claw me.

As I held its still thrashing, dead-but-not-aware-of-it-yet, body up by the neck and the handle my knife provided sticking out of its ribs, I could feel its claws catching on my shirt sleeves, snagging but not tearing; no damage being done to my skin underneath. At least, I was hoping and praying that no damage was being done. I didn't have any choice in the matter though. I had to hold on to the animal until it was dead; otherwise, even though it was injured and dying, it might still try to attack one of us.

The noise it was making was probably the worst part. None of us likes to hear an animal suffer. We've been conditioned almost all our lives to put suffering animals out of their misery if we can't comfort and help them. In this case, I was the cause of the suffering and doing my best to end it quickly. It still sounded horrendous as the animal squealed and howled in pain, all the while trying to sink its teeth into anything it might reach.

It seemed to take forever before the thing started thrashing less violently, even though I knew it was only a matter of a half minute or maybe even less. I made a mental comment to myself about how heavy even a medium sized dog is when you're holding it at arm's length. My shoulders were burning with the effort when the dog finally stopped its squirming, its eyes dimmed, and then closed and its body went limp. Using my grip on its neck and my knife as a lever, I twisted and then wrenched it the other way, using its body weight to pull it off my knife and getting it several yards away from my family.

As my family looked around, maintaining our perimeter awareness and security, I wiped my knife off as best I could on the grass around me and sheathed it before picking up my handgun. I reloaded the handgun and holstered it and then picked up my rifle. I stuffed rounds into the tubular magazine and levered up the first one before declaring myself ready for more travel. Ashley had reloaded her pistol and stowed the empty magazine. Everyone else had reloaded or topped off their magazines as necessary. For sure and certain, surviving in a zombie-outbreak reality had forced us all to become weapons efficient. If you couldn't safely and competently handle weapons in this new reality, you were on the zombie menu. None of us accepted being a meal.

"Moving," I declared as I stepped out. The chorus of acknowledgements confirmed my family's understanding and movement with me in a coordinated fashion. As we walked I thought about the fact that my knife was now potentially infected. I'd have to find a way to sterilize both it and the sheath which, for all intents and purposes, meant boiling both.

I dismissed those thoughts from my mind as we moved through the field. We hadn't gone even a hundred yards when I heard the noise behind us and felt compelled to turn and look. I knew that Dana was back there and would announce any threat, so obviously there wasn't one, but the noise was different and unique and I wanted to see what it was.

I stopped briefly so I could look. My family stopped nearly in unison. As I looked back I gasped at the site I beheld. I'm no stranger to seeing a vulture or buzzard feasting on road kill, but this was awe inspiring. Landing in amongst the scattered bloody remains of the dog pack were more scavenger birds than I had ever seen together at any one time. I had seen as many as ten on a big deer carcass on the roadside, but this… here I saw, at best guess, fifty or more. It was a surprising number.

Perhaps even more surprising was that they didn't appear to fight or compete for the amassed carrion. Their black bodies and wings were so thick in the dog-meat field that I couldn't see any of the dog bodies or blood. All I could see was black scavenger birds. They looked like turkey vultures to me, but I was no bird expert. Then I wondered if birds could carry the zombie virus. If humans could get avian flu (and recent history showed that we could) then it was safe to assume that IF they could carry the zombie virus, they could transmit that to us as well.

As we stood for the moment, several of the large birds looked over at us. I felt a chill of fear at the realization that if this over-large flock of birds decided to attack us, we'd be hard pressed to fight them off. Hitting a moving AND flying target is near impossible, and Dana had the only weapon suited for such an encounter.

With that thought, I turned back to our course and said, "Moving!" My family acknowledged and we kept on going.

We managed to get the rest of the way across the open field, passing the farm house and outbuildings without getting any closer than we absolutely had to. When we reached the next tree line I realized that it would be getting dark soon and before the sun set we wanted to be in a safe camp, fire burning, shelters in place if we could manage it. The last thing we wanted to do, though, was stop and camp the edge of the trees. Further, we didn't want to camp anywhere in the forest. An open field would be best, but I didn't want to back track. I wanted to get as far from the dead dogs and all those vultures as we could.

As we entered the trees I said, "Picking up the pace. Stay alert!" My family acknowledged the statement and, as we worked our way through the trees, spread out just a little more. Once again I felt the awareness of small mammals but was happy not to see any. After we'd been in the trees for about a half hour I heard a horrendous screeching sound going overhead and looked up to see the flock of vultures flying by. Idly I registered the fact that it hadn't taken them long to pick the dog carcasses clean – and then I thanked God that they were flying by and not trying to get down in the trees at us. I didn't know if scavenger birds ever got aggressive but I was sure that, if they did, I didn't want to experience it. We kept moving.

A short while later we emerged from the woods to find ourselves at the fringes of the park I remembered. Part of the park included numerous sports fields: baseball diamonds, soccer/football fields and even some tennis courts. I'd have taken my family onto the tennis courts in a heartbeat because they were all surrounded by twelve-foot-tall chain link fences, but there was no way to set up shelters in the middle. The courts were concrete or whatever hard surface it was, and there were no nets to even use as props, so while the surrounding fence seemed an attractive safety measure, reality was that it hemmed us in and we could set up no shelter unless it was right against the fence.

When the zombie outbreaks had become public knowledge and (finally) government confirmed, the first budget cuts made were to anything recreational. The parks were all overgrown, and none of the sports areas were maintained. As we moved away from the woods and farther into the park's interior, I started scanning for a good place to set up our camp for the night as well as keeping an eye out for any potential threats. For a moment I realized that living on constant alert was very stressful, and I briefly thought about the long term impact it might have on my kids.

Then I realized that, when we were home, the impact of zombies existing wasn't that great. It changed how we lived, but there wasn't a present and ready threat every day. Now that we were traveling and had experienced several unexpected pieces of bad luck (when does anyone ever EXPECT bad luck?), we'd had to improvise and react accordingly. It hadn't been pretty but here we were, still alive and functioning in a healthy, uninfected fashion.

When we reached a point that seemed almost centered in the open space around us, I realized we were in the infield of one of the baseball diamonds. The backstop was what you'd expect: chain link fence at least twelve feet tall on three sides with an even taller wrap over. This field was one of four that made up a rectangle four ball fields long and one ball field wide. Next to the rectangle on one side were football fields. On the other side, the area we'd just walked through was parking lots mixed with picnic areas and what used to be playground space.

I selected the ball field closest to the middle of the triangle and told my family we were going to camp there for the night. Dana and Nate both took good long looks around, assessing the area before agreeing. Johnny just looked unsure and Ashley simply trusted in her parents as most eight year olds do I suppose.

While I stood guard, Johnny, Nate and Dana set up their shelters. It wasn't going to be cold and we dared not get trapped inside of a tent (or tents), so the shelters were slanted tarps tied about four feet high to the fence on one side, and staked down at the corners on the other side. A simple yet efficient lean-to shelter was the result. The boys unrolled their sleeping bags and set their packs in under their shelters. Dana took her sleeping bag and mine and set up a sleeping area using Ashley's zipped open sleeping bag as a mutual cover for the spread.

We didn't want to risk a fire but the night wouldn't be cold so we wouldn't need the heat, and the food we were carrying didn't require cooking. It would certainly taste better if it were warm (MREs are like that) but it could be eaten cold without any problem. I wanted to boil water to clean my knife and sheath but that would have to wait.

Sitting so that we could see all around us, our guns near at hand, each of us tore open an MRE and started in on "dinner." It wasn't the tastiest meal we'd ever eaten, but it was food and it was nutritional... mostly. After dinner I continued to stand guard as Dana made sure each child dug out their travel toothbrush and brushed their teeth.

Throughout the rest of the evening as dusk deepened into night, at least two of us at a time kept a long gun in hand. Everyone else kept their gun close except for Ashley. Her pistol, with the safety on, and secured in her holster, was lying next to her pack under the tarp lean-to. Once night had fully fallen, we went in pairs to visit the porta-johns that still stood in the park. Dana went with Ashley; then Dana and I went; then I went with each of the boys.

Once those nature necessity visits were handled, we sat quietly until the children started to get tired. We agreed on a guard rotation for the night in order of age: Johnny, Nate, Dana and then me. Ashley would get to sleep through the night and the rest of us would deal with it. Silently I wished we could brew some coffee, but we didn't have the grounds and I wasn't building a fire. I told myself to suck it up and then cussed myself mentally before realizing how much conversation I was having *with myself*. I was tired…

19

BRIDGES ARE
FATAL FUNNELS

We got through the night without any incidents. Around "breakfast" the next morning (mostly comprised of protein, power and snack bars) we discussed what each of us had seen or heard during our guard shift. The traffic had continued to pass by on the nearby state road, but it was sparse at best. We did our best to count up how many went by based on memory and came up with a total of less than eight, with six being our best guess. We had each heard the movement of small animals around us in the woods and the sounds of the occasional bird overhead, but none of us actually saw any of them.

Based on how little we'd seen and what our plans were for the morning, I decided we could risk a small fire to make coffee and heat up water to make hot chocolate for Johnny and Ashley. Nate was a "grown up" and considered himself too old (mostly) for something as "childish" as hot chocolate. Having that small fire also meant we could heat up the "breakfast" meat that was contained in one of the MREs. We shared that, did our toiletry visitation routine and then packed up to get moving again.

Back in our travel formation we debated whether we should continue across the park and through the woods or go out to the roadway and move, hopefully more quickly, toward the bridge. Since zombies tend to move through the path of least resistance, we were far less likely to encounter them if we moved through the woods. On the other hand, he would have greater visibility if we were on the road so we'd see any zombies while they were still farther away as compared to when we'd see them in the woods.

Finally the decision was made based purely on assumed travel time. We definitely didn't want to spend another night out if we could avoid it, so our priority was moving as quickly as possible. With that decision made, we headed out of the park along its entrance/exit roadway, and turned west on the state road when we reached it.

I had expected that, with daylight, the traffic on the state road would pick up some, but it didn't seem to very much. Though it would have seemed weird prior to the zombie pandemic, I walked point down the middle of the road. Johnny and Ashley walked about five yards behind me, each on opposite sides of the road. Dana and Nate were in the rear, trailing along another five yards back from Johnny and Ashley. The state, at some time in the past, had cleared three to five yards on either side of the road, so we had that much visual clearance before trees offered potential concealment to anyone or anything. I walked at a steady pace that seemed slow to me but that I knew was pretty quick for Ashley. It took us about a half hour to get close to the river.

On our side of the bridge was an old waterways police station along with a broken-down convenience store and a now-defunct marina. Briefly I thought about the marina as my eyes wandered over the few boats still docked there; some of them floating, some of them partially sunk. I recalled a news report about how many folks had stocked up their boats and taken to the open water to avoid the possibility of zombie attacks. In fact, one cruise line had offered "premium priced passage" on month-long cruises which insured protection from zombie infection... unless one of the passengers was infected. Several cruise ships fell out of radio contact after reporting a zombified passenger. Showing how desperate they were, the closest government ordered the ships sunk by the closest naval or air force component. Maybe some of the smaller boats – yachts I guess you'd call them – offered their families protection, but at some point those people had to come back to land.

All of that flashed through my brain in just a few seconds and certainly my pace never changed in the process. I considered the deserted waterways police station but decided it held no zombie threat. It had likely been abandoned months before and left alone. None of the windows were broken out and the doors I could see were closed; I assumed they were locked.

The convenience store, on the other hand, was half groceries, half liquor, and it had obviously been looted. The windows were all broken out, to include the glass in the main entrance. Trash was strewn in the parking lot around the door, as if dropped by people eating what they stole as they exited the building. A single car sat in the parking lot, its hood up and the passenger side back door open.

Thanks to the parking lots that served those two buildings, the trees were much farther back from the road and I had a clear view of our path of travel all the way to the bridge. Since the bridge was two lanes wide, flat (not arched) and straight, I could see clear to the other side of it. My rising concern was that the bridge was almost a mile long and that was a long way to traverse on such a restrictive and narrow pathway. If zombies caught us while we were on the bridge, we might get caught in the middle of a threat, our only choice to go over the side into the water. The fall into the water wouldn't hurt, but it was a long swim to shore and there was no way we could do it without giving up some weapons.

Then I had a moment of happy realization: each of our go-bags was lined with a waterproof bag. If we tied them right, they would act like big air bubbles inside our packs, turning our go-bags into effective flotation devices. Every member of my family could swim, and with such flotation assistance available, we wouldn't have to surrender our weapons to keep from drowning (think about the weight of everything we were carrying. Without flotation, the guns and ammo alone would sink us like a rock).

I adjusted my path of travel over into the marina area and selected a wide pier as my goal. My family surely had to be curious as to what I was doing but they followed without asking any questions. Idly I realized that we hadn't been passed by even one car, and although it struck me as odd, I was silently thankful that we hadn't encountered any human predators (criminals).

I stopped at the mouth of the long pier, gesturing for my family to come join me. The confused looks on their faces was almost humorous, but, as confused as they were, they were still alert, aggressively looking around with every step they took. It made me proud that as each of them reached me they naturally assumed a defensive position, our cluster ending up about three yards wide as we were all close enough to talk in a conversational voice but none of us was really facing each other; we were all looking out around our 360° perimeter.

"Here's what we're going to do," I said. "We will take turns double checking how the waterproof bags inside our packs are tied. I'll help Ashley with hers. We all know how to tie it so it's airtight. Airtight equals watertight, and we might need the packs as flotation devices. The bridge is longer than I'm happy with, and we can't go across it one at a time. So let's make sure our packs will keep us afloat if, for whatever reason, we end up in the water before reaching the other side."

A chorus of, "Yes, sir," and "Roger that," came back to me.

"Dana, you go first," I said. "Then Nate and Johnny, and I'll help Ashley with hers before doing mine last." I paused and then said, "Go."

The rest of us maintained the perimeter as Dana stepped into the middle of our circle, shrugged out of her pack and started working in it. When she had accomplished her goal she stood up, put her pack back on and assumed a position next to Nate in our perimeter saying, "Done," as she did so. Nate stepped in and started to work on his…

When I heard Johnny said, "Done," and saw him step up next to me I stepped into the middle, happy to note that Ashley did so at the same time I did. She shrugged out of her pack and I double checked her waterproof bag. Helping her back on with her pack, I moved her into position next to Dana and then went to work on my pack.

With it back on, I said "Done," and stepped into the circle facing toward the bridge. Before stepping out I gave a quick briefing. "We move on the bridge just as we did on the road: I'm on point, Johnny and Ashley next, Nate and Mom in the back. We don't go over the side of the bridge unless it's to escape an immediate threat, and no one goes over to help anyone unless the person in the water is asking for help. We don't stop until we're at the other end. Understood?"

The now familiar chorus of "Yes, sir," and "Roger that," came back to me. "Moving," I said and stepped out.

We were half way across the bridge before anything untoward happened. I could hear it long before I saw it. Coming at us from the far end of the bridge was a motorcycle gang. No, scratch that. It was, funny enough, a scooter gang. I felt that was worse. A motorcycle gang, comprised of legitimate tough guys would likely have just passed us by. We wouldn't have much that they would want (except maybe for Dana and Ashley, but I didn't dwell on that thought), but a gang of people riding on scooters would likely have plenty of ego problems and, therefore, plenty they'd want to prove.

I didn't stop walking and glanced back to make sure everyone was keeping up. As the scooters got closer to us, I measured how far we were from the far end of the bridge and guessed the distance at about a quarter mile. Too far to run quickly and easily, and certainly farther than I wanted to swim if we had to go over the side for any reason.

I considered staying in the middle of the bridge but figured it would be just stupid to tempt whoever the scooter gang leader was like that, so I stepped over to one side. The collection continued to slow down behind their leader until he was about parallel with my position on the bridge and then he stopped. I couldn't see any weapons, but virtually every rider was wearing a jacket of some kind so there could have been plenty of handguns or cut-down long guns amongst them.

The leader turned his scooter off, stepped off and lifted off his full-face helmet. He looked to be in his young twenties, looked kind of soft, and was clean shaven. I held my rifle at low ready, not aimed at him, nor even at his feet, but easy enough to get into the fight quickly. I had thumbed back the hammer as he approached, so all I had to do was raise the rifle and fire. I heard Johnny's rifle safety snick off behind me. I would have bet that Nate and Dana had done the same thing but they were too far away for me to hear it.

"Good morning," I said to the leader in a pleasant tone, doing my best to count the scooters and people as I did so. My best guess was about a dozen. They were all stopped now, putting down kick stands and stepping off the motorized small-wheeled contrivances. The leader's response let me know just how bad the day was about to get.

"It was a good morning," he replied. "And then we saw you on our bridge."

Then things seemed to start happening all at once. He started reaching into his jacket at the same time I brought my rifle up into line with his chest and fired. He never even got his handgun out of whatever holster he had it in before the big slug from my rifle punched through his wrist into his chest, the force of it blowing him backward over his scooter.

All around it seemed like the scooter gang members were pulling out an assortment of handguns, and some small part of my mind absently noted that none of them were very impressive. Still, even a cheap small caliber handgun could kill you.

As I levered up the next round in my rifle, I heard a thunderous boom and saw three of the scooter gang members sprout cherry red gouts of blood. I knew that Dana had triggered off a round from her shotgun. The spread had let the nine .32 caliber pellets impact three different targets. Two of them fell. The other one had been hit in the face and arm but was still trying to claw out a handgun. I shot him in the chest and ended his efforts.

The sound of gunfire was a mix of crispy sharp cracks and the deeper booms of my rifle and Dana's shotgun. One of the scooters exploded, and I assumed someone's shot had sparked the gas tank. I levered up my third shot but before I could fire it I realized that the remaining scooter gang members were mounting their "bikes" and high-tailing it away.

Pre-pandemic, when society was still fully functional, I'd have let them drive away. In fact, I'd have been in violation of the law if I had fired at them. Given the conditions post-pandemic, not to mention how angry I was about the clatter of an unnecessary gunfight (brought on by their expanding egos), I shot two of them in the back as they tried to escape. The remaining one, much to my delight, managed to panic and wreck before getting off the bridge.

And then I found myself faced with an ugly conundrum. The bodies of the gang members were strewn around, but I had no way of knowing if any of them were playing possum. I wasn't willing to risk any member of my family by trying to walk through the bodies without being absolutely sure. I loathed the thought of my daughter watching me deliver head-shots to each "corpse," but I couldn't think of any other way to insure our safety.

Carefully lowering the hammer on my rifle to half-cock, I reloaded the magazine to capacity before slinging the weapon. As before, I could hear my family reloading their weapons and felt the reassurance of their competence.

Drawing my handgun, I gave the hand signal to my family to "hold where you are" and then I moved forward into the assortment of bodies. There were eight total and I knew two of them were, for sure and certain, dead. Those were the two whom I'd shot with my .30-.30 at a distance of less than five yards. I could see into their chest cavities and knew their hearts were no longer beating; their lungs no longer drew breath. They were also the closest two bodies to me, so I walked between them as I moved into the corpse assortment.

At the third body I delivered a headshot; and at the fourth, fifth, sixth and seventh. As I approached the eighth body I was all too aware of the fact that I had three rounds remaining in my handgun. I don't know if he heard my footsteps or how he knew I was approaching, but just as I was aiming my handgun at his head, his hand came up with a small revolver in it. The little steel weapon belched flame at the same time my handgun boomed. I was pleased, as I flinched and jumped away to see my shot strike home. Then I realized that I was right at the edge of the bridge, losing my balance, and falling...

Very carefully, very consciously, I engaged the thumb safety on my pistol and jammed it into the holster. Thanks to the holster design, I felt the gun lock in and knew it would not fall out in the water. My rifle was slung, and I had on my pack. I took a deep breath and waited what seemed like forever but was probably one half a second or so to hit the water.

I landed on my back, on my pack, in the water, my body's weight forcing the pack under and following it down. Doing my best not to panic (because panic kills) I unclipped the chest compression strap that helped hold my pack's shoulder straps together on my chest. I then reached down and unbuckled the waist belt and immediately felt the pack start to move away from my body. I had rolled over, and the pack was now above me as the huge air bubble inside of it tried to surface. I crossed my arms in front of my body to make sure I kept the pack on and waited for the surface.

It took only a moment and then I was kicking to right myself. Having the pack on my back and having it be so buoyant was effectively pushing me face down in the water. It took some effort to remain upright, but it was doable and breathing was easy. I realized that the river's current was quickly carrying me away from the bridge, but I wasn't too far from shore – a hundred yards or so – and I started kicking that way. I knew that Dana would take control on the bridge and my family would be waiting for me on shore… somewhere.

I took a minute from swimming toward shore to shrug out of my pack, careful not to lose my slung rifle, and rearrange things so I was on top of the back, wearing it essentially in reverse, my rifle slung across my back. This position meant less effort to keep my face out of the water and it allowed me to swim straight forward, using the breast stroke with the pack holding me up.

As I approached the shore, I saw my family moving down onto the small brown beach, still in a safe formation, each with their weapon held at the ready, their eyes searching for any threat. When the water was shallow enough that I could stand up I did so, rearranged my pack onto my back and unslung my rifle. Dana took one look at my waterlogged clothing and suggested I change clothes. I knew I'd hate myself for it shortly, but I didn't want to take the time to do that. We were less than a half mile from my friend's house and I wanted to get there. We'd be safe there. I could change and put on dry clothes, not to mention wash and dry what I was wearing.

Back in formation, on point and still dripping wet I said, "Moving!" and we started out on the last (hopefully short) leg of our journey to my friend's abode. Thoughts of good food, a shower and dry clothing danced through my head, but not so much as to distract me from paying attention to my surroundings.

20

BODY ARMOR

Thoughts from Travis Anvil Stone

I n general, body armor is a waste of time during a zombie outbreak. Zombies don't use guns. Body armor is cumbersome. Why would you want to wear it? There are two reasons, but they have to be balanced against the weight and discomfort of the body armor itself.

Reason one: During any pandemic, as society begins to falter and collapse, there is an increased threat from our fellow human beings. Those who might have been inclined toward criminal behavior seem to flourish and grow into criminal masterminds in direct opposite ratio to society's downfall. THEY tend to use guns a lot (provided they can find or steal them) and against such a threat, body armor is unquestionably of great value.

Reason two: During a zombie pandemic, if you find yourself in a situation where you are in close quarters contact with a zombie, the body armor can provide greater levels of protection against bites, pokes, gouges and scratches than can normal clothing. Remembering that the zombie infection can be transferred along with just one single cell of a zombie's body, it's best to err on the side of caution all you can.

Those two reasons FOR wearing body armor have to be balanced against the inconveniences of body armor. Those inconveniences include:

- ☣ It's hot. While having an added layer of warmth is great during winter months or in cold climates, it sucks when the temperatures are warm. Added care has to be taken to make sure you don't succumb to heat exhaustion or stroke.
- ☣ It's cumbersome. Even the best and most expensive body armor weighs more than comparable clothing or vests. Carrying that extra weight, no matter how insignificant it may seem at the start, will increase the rate at which you fatigue.
- ☣ It traps and exudes human odor. Where a zombie pandemic is concerned, the last thing you want is to have your human smell stronger than that of all the other humans around you.

In the end, just like with every other piece of equipment and every weapon selection you make, the final choice is yours. I started out wearing body armor when I entered my war against zombies, but in the long run I've learned to carefully weigh when I do or don't wear it. More often than not, if I'm wearing it, it's because of a human criminal threat rather than a zombie threat.

MODERN TECH VS. SIMPLE CHAIN & STEEL

Something else that has to be considered is the modern day technology of body armor versus the "old style" steel mesh or "chainmail." Today's body armor is essentially a weave of fibers that are engineered to have a tensile strength stronger than steel. When projectiles impact these woven super strong layered threads, the weave bends and distorts, absorbing the kinetic energy of the projectile and preventing it from cutting, puncturing or tearing through the ballistic material. Body armor is heavier and thicker in ratio to the speed and weight of the bullet you want it to be able to stop.

Chainmail, on the other hand, is nothing more than links of steel chain hooped together to form a vest, shirt, jacket, leggings, etc. It was originally designed, centuries ago, to stop swords from cutting into or through limbs.

Consider, if you will, the effective value of chainmail against zombie teeth or fingernails. As long as the chain weave is close enough to prevent penetration from those diseased teeth or fingernails, then it's sufficiently effective as a protective garment.

Chainmail MAY be available to you in times or circumstances where contemporary body armor is not. Additionally, if you have the necessary time and tools, along with even just scrap pieces of chain, you can fashion your own chainmail.

Chainmail is not as hot as contemporary ballistic armor because of how open and airy the weave is. It also does not hold body odor so it won't carry around your human scent. It

IS heavy and can be uncomfortable to wear, especially under equipment or gear such as backpacks or gun slings.

Ultimately, you have to decide whether or not you see the need for any type of body armor at all, and if you do, what type offers you the greatest benefits.

21

THE BIGGEST
LESSONS LEARNED

As dictated by Justin Rustovic and notated by Frank Borelli.

It took us about a half hour to get to my friend's house. We approached just as we had traveled on foot, in our formation and spread out so that we couldn't easily all be engaged with a single weapon. I fully expected my friend to see us coming and greet us in some fashion, so I was surprised to find his gate open, his garage door open and no sign of anyone around. Given the number of recent zombie outbreaks, especially the ones that were so close, I was surprised at these security breaches to say the least.

I knew that my family, just like me, was looking forward to some rest and relief from the constant state of alert we'd had to operate under since leaving our truck the day before. While, logically, I knew it had been less than 24 hours, it certainly felt like it had been days. "Combat stress" can do that to you. My concern was, given the circumstances, that my family would relax its guard and there were obviously things out of sorts. We needed to stay alert a short while longer; at least until we could ascertain what had happened here.

"Stay sharp," I said as we approached the fence line. "Let's make sure we can relax before we let our guard down." Verbal acknowledgments all around greeted my ears. I paused for a moment when I was about fifteen yards from the fence line. The gate was wide open. It would be easy to stroll through and approach the house. My mental challenge was that, just as the fence could keep zombies out, it could keep us trapped in there with them if any were inside the perimeter.

I thought for a few moments, weighing options, and then finally just yelled out, "Yo! John!" as loudly as I could. We waited two or three minutes and then I yelled it out again. Neither yell got a response. I considered my next step.

I knew we were going to have to go inside the fenced perimeter and figure out what was going on, or what had happened. My conundrum was how many was 'we' and who it would be. I considered my manpower (my family members), their skill levels, and who had the best chance of survival if one or more of us got killed. Thinking about options and possibilities, I came up with the best plan I could think of.

"Everybody inside the gate," I said. No verbal acknowledgement was required. I stepped through first and kept my rifle trained on John's house as everyone else moved through the gate behind me. Over my shoulder I said, "Latch the gate but don't lock it. Make sure you can get it open in a hurry if you need to."

Again, no verbal acknowledgement greeted me, but I heard the gate swing closed and the latch dropped. "Okay," I said, organizing my thoughts. "Nate and I will clear the house, entering through the garage. One of you needs to stay alert to whatever is outside the fence while the other two watch the house. We'll announce ourselves before coming back out. Consider anyone else suspect."

This time I did get a round of "Rogers" and "Gotchas". I moved out slowly toward the house keeping my rifle in a high ready position. I could feel and hear Nate moving next to me, and a quick glance out of the corner of my eye revealed that he too was moving with his rifle at high ready. It occurred to me that all those months of planning and training with Travis Anvil Stone were paying off in spades.

At the open garage door I slowed a bit to look at what was, or wasn't, there. One vehicle was there, but the other side of the garage was empty. It wasn't used for storage. It was empty as if another vehicle was supposed to be there but was gone. I wondered if maybe John and his family had just gone out? I stole a quick glance out at the fence line and saw that the driveway gate was closed, chain hung around it, lock secured. If they had driven out, why had they locked the driveway gate but left the pedestrian gate open? And why would they leave the garage door open? It made no sense. One of the biggest lessons we had all learned was to *keep your perimeter secure and redundant*. In this case there was a lapse in two levels of their perimeter: the fence and the house.

Sweeping the garage with the muzzles of our weapons as we moved, Nate and I checked behind everything big enough to hide a small child, looked under the SUV still parked, looked inside the SUV and then checked out the storage cabinets John had. They were locked from the outside and I saw no reason to unlock them... yet.

Nate covered our rear as I moved to the door that led into the house. Testing the knob without opening the door I found it unlocked. My confusion built. Leaving the garage door open was breach enough of security protocols, but leaving the door INTO the house unlocked? It was unheard of for anyone who wanted to survive. *Never leave an exterior door or window unlocked* was ingrained into everyone, even by the government survival pundits.

I felt Nate tighten up behind me and knew he was ready to go into the house. Turning the knob, I pushed the door open to the stop and stepped into the house quickly but carefully. Travis had taught us the difference between a dynamic entry, where you enter and move through the house as quickly as you can, engaging every target you find along the way, and a slow and deliberate entry where you move carefully and don't leave a room until you're positive no threat exists anywhere within it. This was going to be a mix. I had no intention of checking every drawer or cabinet, but I would make sure we checked anywhere a zombie could hide. Since even a child could be a zombie, we'd be sure to check cabinets, closets, behind furniture, etc., but we'd do so as quickly as we could visually confirm that no zombies were in hiding. That they even would think to hide still bothered me. All those years of television and movies depicting zombies who were mindless creatures merely moving toward the existence of brains ate at me (no pun intended). That was something else people had learned the hard way: *zombies can think and plan*.

From the garage we had entered the house in the laundry room. Although I felt silly doing so, I checked inside the washer and dryer and found only clothing, either wet or dry dependent on the machine. I checked the laundry supply closet and found the ironing board, a broom and some miscellaneous cleaning supplies. I noted, as an afterthought, the three gallons of bleach and the sprayer. John had apparently practiced another safety protocol. *Always cover your scent* to avoid being hunted.

Going through the laundry room brought us into the kitchen. Nothing looked out of place. All of the knives were still in the butcher block. An empty box sat on one counter, and a check of the cabinets revealed no canned goods… nor any small zombies either. The refrigerator held typical cold items; nothing smelled rotten or spoiled. There was no bottled water, but that didn't mean anything. I don't know why I noted it at that point.

We moved through the family room, formal living room and dining room, careful to check behind any furniture that might conceal anyone. We found nothing. In the front hallway we checked the closet and I noted six empty hangers. That seemed to matter since there were six members of John's family – just like mine.

Going up to the second floor, we checked room by room and found no one… nothing. In one bedroom, a teenager's based on décor, there were dangling cords sitting on the desk, indicating (perhaps) that a laptop computer had been sitting there. A closer look revealed that one of the cords was a charging cord for a cell phone.

I was starting to think that John and his family had abandoned their house. What I couldn't figure out was why and, if they had, why so quickly? I had just spoken to him the day before.

Moving back to the ground floor, we found the stairs to the basement and started down. Half way down the stairs I could see the concrete floor below and, lying on it in a smeared puddle of blood, John's dog. It was a mutt mixture; not a single identifiable breed. What mattered, I realized, was its size. I knew John had always considered his dog too small to be affected by the zombie virus even though he knew the dog could be a carrier.

Looking at the remains of the dog, it was clear that it had, at some point, reached the point in size where the zombie virus did affect it. From what I could tell it looked like John, or some other family member, had used a shotgun to put the animal down. It had obviously been shot more than once and had managed to move/crawl about ten feet before its systems finally were overcome.

I wondered why John and his family had abandoned the house and then I realized: there was no way to safely and totally disinfect/sterilize the basement. Blood splatter and infected-blood-coated pellets from the shotgun shell was on the walls, furniture, etc. In hindsight, I'm surprised they didn't burn the house down on their way out.

Nate and I moved back up the stairs to the kitchen and closed the basement door behind us. There was no way to lock it from either side that I could see, so I wedged a chair under the doorknob and told Nate to keep an eye on it. The last thing we needed was for that zombie dog to somehow reanimate, climb the steps and come at us.

Except for the dog and infection in the basement, the house was safe. John and his family had obviously abandoned it, but he remembered that we were coming so he left us a way in; the open gate and the open garage.

Hanging on a peg in the laundry room was a key labeled for the remaining vehicle in his garage: a mid-size SUV that was large enough to carry us all. Using the luggage racks on top, we could store our gear from our broken down truck. We needed to restock our supplies as best we could.

I called the rest of my family into the house, briefed them on the situation, and then laid out our plan. We would take anything we felt we needed from the ground floor or second floor. John and his family obviously weren't planning on coming back for anything. We'd load up the remaining SUV, go back to our truck, retrieve all we could and then continue on our planned exodus west.

Working as a unit, we packed the empty box on the counter with any food stuffs we could find, especially that wasn't perishable in the short term. John's family had taken most of the dry and canned goods but there were still some good soups, noodles, rice and dehydrated meals on hand. I smiled as I realized that John understood how important it was to *never depend on a refrigeration system to store all your food*.

We couldn't find any bottled water but we did find some unopened water jugs that fed John's water cooler which sat in one corner of the kitchen. Opening a fresh one, we used it to fill some empty squirt bottles obviously meant for the purpose. We loaded all of them and another 5-gallon jug into the back of the SUV. Through the kitchen window I could see John's daisy-chained water barrels and I had to smile again. *Never depend on a single water source. Always make sure your water is purified before drinking or using.*

I knew John kept his ammo in his basement armory and I didn't want to risk going down there at all. Since *every cell of a zombie is infected and infectious*, going down to the basement meant potential contamination. I didn't think we needed ammo badly enough to risk it. Checking to see if I was right, we did an inventory of the ammo we still had remaining for our weapons and reached the mutual conclusion that we were okay. We didn't need to risk the basement.

Since we couldn't think of anything else we needed, and with the SUV loaded with what we'd scrounged, we loaded up, I backed the SUV out of the garage and we lowered the door. I half thought about burning the house down, but when I considered its location, the number and density of trees around it, and the residential population nearby, my concern for starting a forest fire overrode my desire to destroy the contamination in the basement. I wondered if John had come to the same conclusion. As a rule we tried to *never inadvertently kill*

non-infected humans while trying to contain an outbreak or
destroy a contaminated area.

At the driveway gate, Dana, Nate and Johnny all got out. Nate and Johnny opened the gates, unlocking the lock with another key we'd picked up off the laundry room peg board, while Dana maintained guard. I pulled through the open gate, Nate and Johnny quickly closed it and relocked it, and then everyone piled back into the SUV.

The trip back to our broken down truck didn't take even 20 minutes. As we drove back across the bridge we'd walked across earlier, we scattered a flock of turkey vultures that was feasting on the carrion we'd left behind.

At our truck, Dana and Ashley stood guard while the boys and I moved all of our supplies from our truck to John's SUV. We neither saw nor heard anyone or anything as we moved the gear and supplies. John's SUV had about a half-tank of gas, so before we headed out I syphoned all the gas I could out of our truck and into what I was thinking of as our "new truck." I silently wished we had a couple of gas cans because it went against my grain to leave such a valuable energy resource behind. "*Waste not, want not*," was much more than a catchphrase in this new world.

Our trip west took longer than we'd anticipated. Finding supplies along the way was tricky. Every bridge seemed like a new threat. Zombies grew fewer and farther between as we traveled, but we kept going until we finally found what we'd been looking for: a relatively safe stronghold full of confirmed non-infected humans. The community was large and growing as more and more "clean" humans arrived. Each of us was blood tested in a holding area before being admitted.

The leadership in our new home was an elected "council of elders" who ruled humanely but, at the same time, coldly. *Everyone in the community worked*. The children went to school. Everyone over the age of twelve was armed.

As the community grew, so did the secure perimeter around it. *Patrols were made around the community in expanding spirals, looking for infection*; looking for zombies. On the rare occasion one was found, it was immediately destroyed and burned.

Other teams caught and tested small game animals. Those found to be infected were also destroyed and burned. Those found to be clean were brought back into the secure perimeter and domesticated. The community zoo provided for education as well as meat and other food products.

Nate is 18 now; Johnny is 14; Ashley is 10. I do regular work on the external patrols while Dana works on the animal teams. Nate is training to be part of the community defense force while Johnny is eager to join the community's search and rescue teams.

As I look back, I have to be thankful for the lessons we learned from Travis Anvil Stone. What he taught us, though so much of it seemed silly at the time, proved to be invaluable. Following those lessons brought us safely to where we are and will see us (hopefully) safely into the future.

Writing from a secured and protected location, this is Justin Rustovic… out.

ABOUT THE AUTHOR

Frank Borelli is a military service veteran with experience as a Military Policeman, an Infantry soldier and a Combat Engineer. In addition to his military service, he's spent all of his adult life – approximately 30 years as this text is prepared – working in law enforcement and training officers/deputies how to survive high-risk situations.

This book marks his eighth published book: five non-fiction, two fiction and one mixed, in addition to two research papers that have been published.

Frank accepts emails with comments, criticisms and observations to frankborelli@officer.com.